# An Amish
# Family
# Christmas

D1115667

# An Amish Family Christmas

Murray Pura

HARVEST HOUSE PUBLISHERS
EUGENE, OREGON

*Cover by Garborg Design Works, Savage, Minnesota*

*Cover photos © Chris Garborg; Bigstock/gnagel*

**AN AMISH FAMILY CHRISTMAS**
Copyright © 2013 by Murray Pura
Published by Harvest House Publishers
Eugene, Oregon 97402
www.harvesthousepublishers.com

Library of Congress Cataloging-in-Publication Data
    Pura, Murray
    An Amish family Christmas / Murray Pura.
        pages cm.
    ISBN 978-0-7369-5237-8 (pbk.)
    ISBN 978-0-7369-5238-5 (eBook)
    1. Amish—Fiction. 2. Christmas stories. I. Title.
    PR9199.4.P87A45 2013
    813'.6—dc23

                                                                2013010154

**Printed in the United States of America**

13  14  15  16  17  18  19  20  21 / BP-CD / 10  9  8  7  6  5  4  3  2  1

*For Nana Doede, who loves all my stories,*
*with all my love.*

# One

Naomi glanced out the window as one black buggy followed another along the lane leading away from the house. Rain streaked the glass and distorted the shapes of the wheels and the horses' heads. One part of her felt nothing as she watched them leave, another part felt as gray as the Lancaster County sky, and a third part began to count the buggies as if she were a child again and learning her numbers.

*Seven, eight, nine, ten, eleven.*

"I've made us some tea." A young woman in a dark dress and dark bonnet stood at her side.

"*Danke.* I don't know if I can drink, Rebecca."

"Of course you can drink." The young woman took Naomi's hand gently but with a measure of strength. "Come sit by the fire."

Naomi took a chair on one side of the woodstove, and Rebecca took a chair on the other side. The stove had a glass pane that allowed them to see the yellow flames curling up and over the wood. Nearby, a box of split logs stood ready to feed the fire. A small table between them held a teapot, cups, and a plate of biscuits. Naomi gazed at the fire but made no effort to pour herself any tea, so Rebecca did it for her, handing her a cup and offering the plate of biscuits.

Naomi took the cup but shook her head at the plate. "I can't."

"Try."

"I can't, Rebecca."

Rebecca put the plate down on the table and curled her fingers around her own cup of tea. Neither of them spoke. When the fire began to turn into red coals, Rebecca got up and placed several more pieces of wood inside the stove, closing the door tightly. Flames leaped up orange and white.

"Two weeks before Thanksgiving." Naomi hadn't taken a sip from her teacup. "What kind of Thanksgiving will it be? What kind of Christmas?"

"The church will be at your side. I'll be there. You won't be alone."

"My family is gone."

"Luke is with you."

Naomi lifted her head sharply and stared at her friend. "Luke? Luke is with me? Luke is catatonic. Who knows but God where Luke is?"

"He won't be that way forever."

"He won't? How do you know that? The doctors say the odds in his favor are less than twenty percent."

"I'm praying. The whole community is praying."

"Yes? And praying for the drunk who drove into our buggy too?"

"Of course, Naomi," Rebecca said quietly. "It's our way."

"He kills my father and mother and sister and leaves my twenty-year-old brother half dead in the ditch. Drives away. Doesn't even call nine-one-one. For all we know my sister or mother could have been saved."

"Hush. I know."

Naomi had been looking for an argument for days and had finally found it. Her eyes blazed black fire. "You know? But all you can think of to do is pray for the murderer?"

"What else should I do? Throw his children under a Percheron's hooves so there can be even more death and suffering?"

Naomi gazed at the flames. "He will have a fine Thanksgiving. Sit down to a fine meal at Christmas. All the chairs at his table will be occupied. His whole family will break bread with him."

"It does no good to dwell on such things. God has a plan."

Naomi snapped up her head, and her eyes flared. "A plan? This is his plan? To snatch away my family in a heartbeat and leave me alone and broken?"

"You are not alone. I will help you. Your husband's family will help you."

Naomi's eyes returned to the fire. "I have no husband."

"Shh now." She smiled gently. "If you have no husband, then I have no brother. He binds you and me together, Naomi. Our family is now your family. We will take you in."

"I do not wish to be taken in. I'm staying in this house. I'm going to die in this house."

Rebecca raised her eyebrows. "This big farm? You're going to run it on your own?"

"Yes. I have two hands and a strong back."

"You can't undertake such a thing. Especially once Luke returns from the hospital and you have to care for him."

"I can do it."

"It's too much."

"I'm going to do it. The church can help me or not help me. God can help me or not help me."

"Of course God and the church will help you."

Naomi had both hands around her cold teacup. She dropped her head. "I'm not ungrateful. But I'm staying here in this house. It's my home on earth."

Rebecca gazed at her and finally nodded. "Very well." She got to her feet. "Bishop Fischer said Luke would be home by next

Wednesday. There's nothing more they can do for him in town, and the care is expensive."

"I know that."

"So I'm going upstairs to clean and tidy his room."

Naomi rubbed her forehead with her hand. "I haven't touched it since the accident. I haven't even opened the door to look inside. I haven't looked in any of the rooms—not Mama and Papa's, not Ruth's—"

Her voice broke, the cup fell from her fingers and shattered on the hardwood floor, her body began to convulse, and loud cries came from her throat. "*Mein Gott, mein Gott, warum hast du mich verlassen!*"

Rebecca rushed over and threw her arms around Naomi. "No, no, he hasn't forsaken you. He is with you. It's the valley of the shadow of death, but he remains by your side. He is here."

"I don't feel him here," sobbed Naomi. "I don't feel his presence."

"He is with you. He who wept at his friend's grave is with you."

"I thought…I heard his voice at the funeral…but no, it was the wind, only the wind…"

Rebecca rocked her. "Hush. You're exhausted, worn out with grief. You have not slept."

"There was nothing. Only the clouds and the rain and the wind in the grass. Nothing else. Nothing, Rebecca."

―∽∾―

Naomi eventually steeled herself and helped Rebecca, her sister-in-law and friend, clean and tidy the rooms of her parents and sister and Luke. The next day the families in the Amish community brought meals for the two women as well as jars of preserves of meat and fruit and vegetables. The day after that, *Englisch* families did the same thing. Rebecca remained by her side the entire time, sleeping in a spare room, eventually bringing over her clothing and settling in, determined that Naomi shouldn't be alone. Naomi protested the first two days. After that she didn't protest at all. She didn't talk about it, but inside, where her pain and grief and desolation twisted around her soul with sharp spikey thorns and black vines, the only things that gave her relief were long bouts of prayer, gold and crimson sunrises, and Rebecca's gentle but strong presence.

Bishop Fischer and the ministers hired a driver with a van to take themselves and Naomi and Rebecca to the hospital and back. Two doctors spoke with them for half an hour. Nothing new was said. Naomi sat with her cold-weather bonnet on her head, her hands clasped in the lap of her black dress, eyes focused on the doctor's shoulders as she rehearsed his instructions.

*Catatonic stupor. Deficit of motor activity. Such activity may in fact be reduced to zero. Luke will avoid bathing. He will avoid caring for his hair or nails. He will not make eye contact. Sometimes mute. Sometimes rigid. Sometimes flexibility that is out of the ordinary. No attempt to socialize. Extreme negativity. May refuse food and drink— if this occurs he will have to return to the hospital for an IV. Benzodiazepine must be administered regularly. Excellent chance he will respond to the BZD regimen. The exact causes of catatonia are unknown. In his case we speculate head trauma from the accident. Keep his room dimly lit and peaceful. Don't be discouraged. Patients suffering from catatonia often respond swiftly to medication. A family setting is a positive influence and may help him on the road to recovery. Keep in touch.*

⁓⌒⁓

"Here you are, Luke."

Naomi stood with her brother outside the door to their home. The bishop and ministers and Rebecca were behind them.

"Can I help you to your room?"

Luke didn't respond. His pale blue eyes were far away from her.

She took his hand. It was like holding a rock. Slowly she tugged him up the steps to the porch and drew him into the house. She gently coaxed him up the staircase to his bedroom. His eyes didn't even flicker when he saw his bed and books. He had loved to read since he was a boy, but now he showed no interest in the three or four dozen volumes or anything else in his room.

"Would you like to lie down, Luke? Are you tired? Perhaps a nap would help you feel better."

Luke made no move toward his bed. He remained at his sister's side, silent and rigid as stone.

"How about your chair? The one you like to sit in when you read?"

Luke didn't respond.

Rebecca was at the door. Naomi turned to her. "Will you help me get him into his chair? I want to prepare a hot lunch for him, and it would be better if he were sitting up."

"Of course."

Together they led Luke to the burgundy armchair with its large armrests and large soft seat and back. Getting him to bend his knees and lower himself into it was almost impossible, for he would not cooperate. Finally Rebecca placed her hands on his chest and pushed him, and he fell back, his knees flexing despite himself. There he sat like the statue of a man on a throne.

Her eyes dark and large, Naomi looked at him. "I'm going to fix your favorite chicken soup, Luke. The one with the dumplings. All right?"

Luke stared straight ahead.

"Will you sit with him, Rebecca?" she asked.

"I will."

"I'll bring soup and some of Mrs. Yoder's sourdough rye for you as well as him."

"*Danke.*" Rebecca smiled. "I should like that. Hot food cheers me up."

The bishop and ministers were in the hall outside the room.

"Daughter, let us pray for you," Bishop Fischer said.

Naomi bowed her head. The men had already removed their broad-brimmed black hats when they entered the house.

The bishop prayed in High German. He asked that God bless the home and all who dwelled in it. He asked that Luke be healed and speak and laugh as he had done so easily less than two weeks before. He asked that Naomi be touched in a very special way. All the ministers prayed. Then Bishop Fischer concluded with a plea, his voice rising, his tone almost desperate.

"*Mein Gott, wir brauchen einen Ihrer Wunder.*"

"Yes, God, we need one of your miracles," whispered Naomi. "No matter what it looks like, no matter how it comes, no matter how strange or unusual it appears. Even if I don't recognize it. Even if I don't believe it. Come, Lord Jesus. Come to us in whatever manner you wish. Please. I cry out to you. Amen."

The bishop heard her words. His eyes met hers as she raised her head.

"Amen," he repeated. He and the ministers left, the harnesses on their horses jingling as the buggies pulled away from the house.

The soup was not a great success. Half of it dribbled down Luke's chin.

*But the other half went into his mouth and into his stomach,* Naomi told herself.

They helped Luke into his bed that night, and Naomi got him into his pajamas while Rebecca washed dishes downstairs. Naomi found she couldn't sleep because she was thinking about him constantly, so she finally took a blanket and pillow and went to his room. The candle showed her that his eyes were closed, and she could hear his breathing, deep and even.

*That is something. Thank you, God, for his sleep.*

She curled up in the chair with her pillow and blanket and quickly fell asleep herself.

In the morning she shaved him and washed his body with a cloth and soap and a basin of warm water. He wouldn't take the hash browns she offered him or the muffins or the eggs fried sunny-side up the way he liked. But he did drink a mug of coffee with cream and sugar in slow sips.

*That also is something. Not much, but something. Thank you for this.*

Feeling more tired than she had in days, she left him sitting up in his chair, staring at the wall, and went down to clean the kitchen with Rebecca. She carried the plate of eggs and hash browns and the empty coffee cup.

"No to that as well?" asked Rebecca, whose arms were up to their elbows in suds as she washed dishes in the sink.

"*Ja*," replied Naomi wearily. "But at least the coffee he tried."

"And he drank it all? Or only some?"

"All."

Rebecca smiled. "Good. He will make it then. Many of the men I know live on coffee and nothing else in the mornings."

For the first time in weeks Naomi gave a short laugh. "*Ja*. This was true of Papa."

But the memory brought a dagger with it that pierced her moment of light. Rebecca saw Naomi's face fall into lines of darkness as she picked up a dishtowel and began to dry plates and forks.

"I can do this," Rebecca protested.

But Naomi carried on as if her friend had never spoken.

*My Lord, I feel like I myself am dead.*

"Who is that?" asked Rebecca looking out the window.

Naomi kept her head down, drying a cup. "Someone with a meal?"

"No, it looks like…a soldier."

Surprised, Naomi looked out into the farmyard. "A soldier? What would a soldier be doing here?"

He was in a desert uniform and carried a duffel bag over his shoulder.

Ice shot through Naomi, and she put her knuckles to her mouth.

Rebecca stared at the man as he made his way to the door. "Oh, Naomi, I can't believe it!"

"It's your brother." Naomi continued to gaze out the window, dishtowel and cup still in her hands. "Rebecca, it's your brother."

Rebecca glanced at her sharply. "And your husband."

"No." Naomi shook her head. "No. I don't have a husband anymore."

A tear cut across Rebecca's cheek. "It doesn't matter what you say. He *is* your husband. And God has brought him home alive from the war."

# Two

"Micah!"

Rebecca, her hands and arms still wet from the dish-washing, threw open the door and ran into his arms. He dropped his duffel bag and gathered her in, kissing her on the cheek.

"I can't believe it!" She hugged him as tightly as she could, tears on her face. "Praise God! We knew nothing about how you were, nothing!"

"I wrote. I wrote you all. Every week."

"But we never saw the letters. We were not permitted to see the letters."

He kissed the top of her head, holding her closely. "I know. It's all right. I'm home now."

"Mama and Papa will want to see you."

"I went to our house first thing and spent an hour with them. Then I walked to the bishop's place and spent another hour with him."

"The bishop?" Rebecca pulled back to look at his face and eyes. "And how was that?"

"We talked over everything just like we did a year ago. He told me he thanked God that I had come home alive but that nothing has changed as far as the church is concerned. I'm still to be shunned for going to war…if I don't repent."

"And he knows you're here talking with me? That you spoke with Mother and Father and our brothers and sisters?"

"*Ja.* I have three days to repent. If I don't, the *bann* is back in force."

Micah looked at Naomi, who was standing in the doorway. "Hello."

"Hello," she replied.

"It's been a long time."

"Yes."

"I wrote you every chance I could."

"You knew I wouldn't be permitted to see the letters."

"Someone must have them. There are more than fifty."

Naomi dropped her eyes. "What good did it do to make the effort? I asked you not to go to war and you did anyway. You knew how hard it would be on me."

"On both of us," Micah said quietly, leaving his sister and walking toward the door.

"It's the same old argument. You wanted the war more than you wanted me. Or our way of life."

"I didn't want the war. I wanted to save the lives of the men in the war, friends and foes. I went as a medic and I wanted you to understand that."

"Well, I didn't understand a year ago and I don't understand today. So what's the point of our getting together again?"

"You are my wife."

"That made no difference to you when you enlisted."

Micah put his hands in the pockets of his desert uniform. "The bishop asked that we resume living together. But we're not to eat with each other or share the same bed or have any relations with one another, and I may not attend worship services or do business with anyone in the Amish community. I can work the farm, and we can sit under the same roof."

"And never talk."

"Not after Sunday, no."

"Unless you repent."

Micah shook his head. "Naomi, how do you expect me to stand before God and tell him I'm sorry I saved the lives of hundreds of men and women—American, Canadian, British, Dutch, Afghan? How could I honestly say that to him and mean it? I didn't take life, Naomi, I gave it back to those who had almost lost it. I gave it back in the name of God and Jesus Christ. You want me to say that was wrong?"

Naomi didn't reply.

"This isn't how I wanted our first meeting to begin." Micah's voice grew soft, the softness she remembered. "I'm here because my combat tour ended and I've been discharged. I knew nothing of the accident that took the lives of your parents and Ruth. I'm so sorry. God himself knows how sorry I am. I may have left here because I felt the Lord wanted me to bind up the wounds of the fallen. I may have enlisted and been shunned by our people. But when I left, I left loving your family. They knew that."

Naomi's eyes were still lowered. "Yes, they did."

"I left loving you."

She was silent.

"I wanted you to understand," he almost whispered.

"Understand what?" Her voice took on a sharp edge. "What did you expect me to understand?"

"That I couldn't sit back and watch soldiers and civilians being killed without doing something about it. That I needed to do my part to ease the pain and suffering. That I needed to heal like Jesus healed. That I felt it was a calling in my heart from God."

"But you are Amish."

"I didn't kill."

"You helped the war effort."

"I helped women and men and children return to their homes alive. That was the effort I made. I love you so much, Naomi. I need you to understand that was the effort I made."

Again she didn't know what to say to him.

After a moment he asked, "Where's Luke?"

"Upstairs in his room."

"I'm going to look in on him."

Naomi lifted her face. "He won't know you. He won't speak."

"In three days you won't speak to me again, so what is the difference?"

Micah brushed past her and went into the house and up the staircase. Naomi and Rebecca looked at each other.

Rebecca shrugged. "How can we argue with him? Everything he says sounds right."

"Not for an Amish man."

"But God is not an Amish God, is he? He is everyone's God. How can I say the Lord didn't put in his heart this desire to save people from the bombs and bullets of war?"

Naomi glanced away. "Let's finish the dishes."

"I should go."

"Why?"

"Because your husband has returned, and you need to live with him in this house, not me."

Naomi made a face. "Some life. We'll be like ghosts to one another. How can I ask him to help me with Luke when I can't even explain to him what I want?"

Rebecca bit her lower lip. "I feel out of place."

"Please don't go. It's going to be hard enough without losing you too."

"You're not losing me."

"You'll be a mile away. Of course I'm losing you."

Rebecca folded her arms over her chest. "Well, I'll speak with Micah about it. And my parents. And the bishop. Let us see what they will say about such an arrangement."

Naomi nodded. "All right."

"Until then I will remain here with you."

Naomi smiled. "*Danke*."

Rebecca offered her a small smile in return. "*Bitte*." She came over and took her friend's hand. "And I'll be praying for you, *ja*, for you and my brother. He has come home alive. This should be a happier day for you, my sister by marriage and by God."

"Of course I'm happy to see that he's alive. I just don't know what to do. I'm an Amish wife but he's not an Amish husband."

"Are you sure?"

"He won't repent, so the shunning will continue. How Amish is that of him to keep doing this to our marriage?"

"Let's pray about all of it and see what God will do. It may be that my brother isn't the only one who has to budge on this."

Naomi's eyes widened. "What? Me? What can I do? Agree with him so that we're both expelled from the church?"

"I'm not thinking of you. I'm thinking of the bishop and the ministers."

"Them? When do they ever change their minds?"

"Let's wait and see. Meanwhile, I hope you have enough feelings left in your heart for my brother that you can embrace him and welcome him home."

Naomi passed a hand over her eyes. "I don't know what I'm able to do. Micah and I haven't talked in a year. We haven't been able to write. Now my family is gone and he is here, but I still feel utterly alone."

"Well, try a hug anyway. It can't hurt."

"I think it can."

They both went back into the house as Micah came down the staircase. His face had tightened, and its lines had deepened.

"What's Luke's prognosis?" he asked Naomi.

"Prognosis?" she responded. "You sound like a doctor."

"That's the way I've sounded for the past year. Is he on medication?"

"*Ja.*"

"BZD?" asked Micah.

"*Ja.*"

"Do they connect the onset of the catatonia with head trauma from the accident?"

"They say they understand so little about catatonic states. They can only guess."

"Well, if a person is fine before an accident and has catatonia immediately afterward, I think it's a good guess. What's become of the drunk driver?"

"His trial is set for the spring. He can't leave the state."

"So…"

"So he's home with his family and getting ready for Thanksgiving."

"And you were at home when the accident occurred?"

"*Ja.*"

Micah nodded, turning over what she had just told him. Then he went to a closet by the door and took a dark winter coat off a peg. It was at least a size too small, but he pulled it on over his uniform. A broad-brimmed black hat that had belonged to Naomi's father went on his head. It also was too small, but he left it on.

"What are you doing?" asked Naomi.

"I'm going to pay my respects to your mother and father and Ruth." He paused as he opened the door. "Would you like to join me?"

"Oh, I don't think so, no."

Rebecca shot an annoyed glance at her, but Naomi ignored it, picking up the dishtowel and returning to the plates and cups.

Through the window the two young women could see Micah

leading the black gelding, Maria, from the barn and harnessing her to the buggy. He spent a moment talking to the horse, stroking the side of her neck until she nickered and bent her head to tug at his coat with her teeth. After that he climbed up into the driver's seat.

Words suddenly made their way into Naomi's mind, words and strong memories of her wedding ceremony.

*"Do you have confidence, brother, that the Lord has provided this, our sister Naomi, as a marriage partner for you?"*

*"Ja."*

*"Do you also have confidence, sister, that the Lord has provided this, our brother Micah, as a marriage partner for you?"*

*"Ja."*

*"Do you also promise your wife that if she should in bodily weakness, sickness, or any similar circumstances need your help, you will care for her as is fitting for a Christian husband, Micah?"*

*"Ja."*

*"Do you promise your husband the same thing, Naomi? That if he should in bodily weakness, sickness, or any similar circumstances need your help, you will care for him as is fitting for a Christian wife?"*

*"Ja."*

*"Do you both promise together that you will with love, forbearance, and patience live with each other and not part from each other until God will separate you from death?"*

*"Ja."*

Naomi dropped the dishtowel and ran to the door, flinging it open.

"Micah! *Warten Sie eine Minute! Ich komme mit dir!*"

He pulled back on the reins, and the mare came to a stop.

"*Sind Sie sicher?*" he asked her. *Are you sure?*

"*Ja, ich bin mir sicher.*"

She pulled on her coat and wrapped a dark scarf about her throat.

"You'll keep an eye on Luke?" she asked Rebecca as she pulled on woolen gloves.

"Of course."

"I'm not sure when we'll be back."

"Take all the time you need."

"All the time we need? We need a lifetime."

Naomi rushed out the door and strode across the farmyard to the buggy, her head erect, her back straight. Micah watched her come and waited, the leather traces in his hands. Rebecca saw her say something to Micah, one gloved hand on the side of the buggy. Then she climbed in beside him.

Not for the first time or the last time, Rebecca marveled at the beauty God had bestowed on the slender, dark, and flashing-eyed woman who was Naomi Miller by birth and Naomi Bachman by marriage. But along with the beauty, he had also bestowed a fiery temper and a backbone as stubborn and unyielding as steel.

"I have no idea how you are going to bring the two of them together again, Lord," Rebecca whispered as the buggy rolled down the lane to the road. "But you made the marriage, and you put the desire to be a medic in Micah's heart, so it's your problem. All I can do is pray and remind you of that."

# Three

The day had been astonishing enough already with Micah's return from Afghanistan. Now Naomi witnessed something else just as astonishing. Micah walked ahead of her into the plain cemetery of plain gray stones and plain brown grass, found the fresh mounds of earth at her family's graves, knelt by them, and wept. And not just any sort of weeping. It was loud and sharp, and it covered his face with tears and seemed to come from the pit of his soul.

Naomi herself began to cry just watching him and listening to his pain. He had been close to Ruth and her mother and father, but she had no idea he would feel the loss so deeply. Now and then he had shed a tear in the year of marriage they had enjoyed before he enlisted, but nothing like this. She didn't know if she should touch his shoulder or kneel beside him or speak a word of comfort or what she should do. So she went back and sat in the buggy and prayed and waited.

*This man I married is a stranger to me. I do not know him. I do not understand him.*

She watched as he stood and searched the pockets of her father's winter coat for a handkerchief. He found a white one, unfolded it, and wiped his eyes and cheeks as he made his way back to the buggy. Climbing up beside her, he said nothing. He shook the reins, and Maria pulled them back onto the road. He was staring straight ahead when the words came, and there were not many of them.

"You don't know how it feels to think you were thousands of miles away saving the lives of people you'd never known but totally unaware the ones you loved most were dying in a wreck at the side of a highway."

He took them down a side road and stopped at the house they had lived in for a year before he left to join the army. It was white and simple, two stories, nothing to distinguish it from countless other houses scattered up and down the roadway except that its windows were boarded up with large sheets of plywood.

"What did you do with our beef cattle?" he asked her.

"Papa took care of them as you wished. They're in a pen he built about three hundred yards behind the house."

"They never roam free as they did with us?"

"*Ja*. Papa had a long fence built around our acreage so they could do that."

"I suppose that was expensive."

"Not at all. Men from the church had it up in a few days. Mr. Zook supplied the lumber free of charge."

Micah looked from the house to her. "No wire?"

She decided to meet his gaze. "No wire. Papa detested wire. He hated when animals got snagged on it."

His eyes lingered on hers. "You've grown more lovely in my absence."

"Don't say that." But she didn't look away.

"Why shouldn't I say that?"

"Because you've been gone too long. And you've been silent too long."

"No, Naomi, I've not been silent. There wasn't one letter I wrote you where I didn't say how I ached to gather you up in my arms and hold you close enough to smell the soap you use on your skin and the gentle scent you use on your hair."

"Stop it."

"Who has the letters? Bishop Fischer? Or did your father keep them in a drawer in his desk? If you opened one of them you would know I have longed for you every day I was away from you."

She dropped her eyes. "Well, I will never be able to read them."

"So then I'll tell you how I feel now that I'm here."

"Until they order us to cease speaking to one another Sunday night."

"My eyes will tell you all you need to know."

"Micah—"

"I saw hundreds of desert sunrises and desert sunsets, Naomi. None of them more beautiful than the beauty God has put in you."

She kept her eyes down. "You shouldn't say such things."

"I'm your husband. I'm your lover. Who else should say such things?"

She couldn't think of a retort or any sort of response.

"Where is my clothing?" he asked after a moment.

"I stored it at our house. In the room you will use."

"What room is that?"

"Well, the room where I've put the broken things to be fixed. Your sister has the other spare room."

Micah laughed. "So who will come and fix me? You? God? The bishop?"

"None of this is funny."

"I disagree, Omi, this is very funny." He used the pet name she hadn't heard since his enlistment. "What are you going to stick me in with? Busted clocks? Cracked sinks? Chairs without seats? Porcelain figurines that need to be glued?"

She tried unsuccessfully to hold back a smile. "There is a cuckoo clock, *ja*. The farmer and his Percheron won't come out at noon to look around."

"I remember the clock. Well, I'll squirrel away with my tools and a bottle of glue and spend my evenings repairing him and his friends. Soon enough he'll be eager to come out like any Amish farmer and see what I've done. Old Moses Fischer, he comes to mind."

Naomi imagined the bishop's father and couldn't stop her smile. "Shh."

"Why, with the right bottle of glue and a pair of strong clamps I think I could fix Old Moses up right as rain too."

"Oh, hush." She put a hand to her mouth and her eyes crinkled. "I don't want to laugh and you're making me laugh."

"That's good to hear."

"A year you've had to grow up and you're still a crazy boy."

"*Ja, ja*, crazy, that's me."

Their eyes came together again and the rich golden brown in his made something hard and stiff and full of edges vanish inside her.

She looked away from him. "I made up my mind I wouldn't be kind to you or intimate with you. But now all I can think of is that I haven't seen your eyes or heard your laugh for a whole year. Your arms haven't been around me and you haven't unpinned my hair in the slow and careful way you like to do. I'm a failure at keeping you away from me."

She reached out a hand and awkwardly stroked his cheek as if she were a teenage girl touching a boy for the first time. "I wish you could come to some sort of agreement with the bishop and the ministers. I can't bear the thought of having you under my roof and not being able to touch you. It's already been more than twelve months. Oh, Micah, it will be an agony. Can you not make peace with the leadership?"

He put his lips to the palm of her hand as she stroked his skin. The kiss made things move around inside her.

"Not unless they wish me to be unfaithful to myself and to my God," he replied.

"Micah, I can't endure another season of silence with you. I really cannot."

"I pray it won't be a long season."

"What makes you say that? You're stubborn, they're stubborn… it could last a thousand years."

"It won't. You know it won't. God will do something. He's the only one who can be a just arbitrator in this business."

She almost gasped. "God will do something? For him one day is as a thousand years! Why don't *you* do something instead?"

"What would I do?"

"I don't know. Repent. Change the rules. Fix the bishop with your tools and your glue."

Micah smiled. "There *is* something I can do. Steal a kiss."

Her face reddened as if she were a schoolgirl. "Steal a kiss? We're not to have any relations."

"I asked the bishop if I could be permitted a welcome home kiss."

"And what did he say?"

"Bishop Fischer waved his hand in the air as if it were not a big thing. '*Ja, ja,*' he told me, 'kiss, kiss.' So that gives me at least two kisses under the *Ordnung*. Though I'm pretty sure I get more because I think his 'kiss, kiss' is plural…you know, that it means as many kisses as I like."

The smile crept over Naomi's mouth again. "That's what you think."

He shrugged and reached out to brush his thumb over the full redness of her mouth. His touch sent an electric shock through her from head to foot.

"*Ja,* that's what I think," he replied. "Come, let Maria take us around to the back of the house where the Zooks and the Harshbergers don't have eyes."

She kissed his thumb. "You make me feel like I'm sixteen."

"*Ja*? Well, I intend to do something that will fortify you until this whole enlistment and shunning controversy is put to bed and settled."

"Fortify me? What do you have in mind?"

"You'll see."

He steered the buggy along their lane and behind the house. Now all that could be seen were acres of dry brown hayfields. Gently he removed her dark bonnet and drew the pins out of her hair one by one.

"A woman's crowning glory is her hair," whispered Micah. "Paul knew what he was talking about."

"You're going to quote the Bible to me now?"

"Of course, why not?"

"I think Paul meant if a woman had abundant hair it was a glory to her for it covered her head."

"I could start with the Song of Solomon if you wish."

"Oh, stop. You make me blush."

"Your hair is just like a shining night. There's scarcely any difference. You have no idea how many times I wrote that in my letters. You have no idea how many times I looked up at the desert stars far away from the bright lights of Kandahar and thought of how your hair moves through my fingers and how it flows over your shoulders and down your back at bedtime. Thinking of you was like fire eating me up. You consumed me, Naomi, you took everything."

"Hush. Don't exaggerate so."

"I'm not exaggerating." Her dark hair was loose over her neck and dress as he took her face in his hands. "How I love you. How I thank God for you, my bride."

Tears cut down her cheeks. "I feel the same way…oh, I feel the same way. Forgive me for holding back, forgive me for not welcoming you home with a hug and a kiss."

"Welcome me now, Naomi Bachman."

His mouth came down over hers. She responded by returning the kiss with a surge of passion. He rejoiced in the farm-girl strength of her arms and hands as she held him tight. He poured all the long nights into his kiss, all the desert heat, all the danger, all the fear that he would never see her again, the death, the dying, the wounded he saved and the wounded he couldn't save, the tears, the pain…everything from a war ten thousand miles away that had cut him in two. When they finally gently released each other, he touched his lips to her long hair, to her throat, to the curve where neck and shoulder met, back to her eyes, her cheeks. He pried her hands away from him and covered them with kisses, he drank in her scent and her warmth, and it was never enough, it had been too long.

"Micah." She pulled back with a gasp. "If you keep this up there will be nothing left of me."

"I want you fortified for the weeks ahead."

"Fortified? I have no reserves left. You haven't fortified me. You've besieged me."

"So you surrender?"

"I surrender."

"I was saving all of it up for an entire year."

"*Ja*, it feels like that."

"It is like that." He glanced at the back door of the house and the sheet of plywood that covered it. "If I were free to do so I would tear the board off that door and carry you inside."

"Oh, it would be cold inside, Micah."

"Not for long."

"Make peace with the leadership, and I will let you do that."

"I would start a fire in the stove first, believe me."

"Why bother?"

He smiled. "So now my mischievous Amish Annie is back. How long will she stay?"

Naomi traced her finger over his lips. "Forever. I still don't understand why you did what you did, but you're my man, my husband, and I love you."

"What did you say?"

She laughed. "I said I loved you."

"If we have come that far that fast, it calls for another kiss."

Naomi pushed him back with both hands. "Oh no you don't. We need to get back and see how your sister is getting along with Luke. And I need to pin my hair up."

"I can help with that."

"Oh, sure, you can help! I put one pin in and you pull out two!" She took a hand off his chest and lifted a finger in warning. "Keep your eyes out for gossips and give me three minutes."

Micah leaned back with a smile on his face. "And what exactly do you want me to do if I see gossips?"

"Push my head down so they don't see me and then wave to them."

"Ah, wave to them. Do you think they will wave back to a soldier?"

Naomi had her hands up in her hair, gathering it at the back of her head, pins in her mouth. "They don't know you're a soldier," she mumbled with difficulty.

"But if they recognize my face they'll know. I don't think there's a welcome for soldiers here."

Her eyes were a strong dark brown as she looked at him, putting the finishing touches to her hair. "Your sister and your mother and father have welcomed you. Your wife has welcomed you. It took her a while, *ja*, but she finally did the right thing. The Lord alone knows—the day may arrive when the whole Amish community will welcome you home with open arms."

"You don't really think that, do you, Naomi?"

She fastened her prayer *kapp* back on her head. "A day ago I would have said no. Two hours ago I would have said no. Now something in me says *ja*."

"Something in you says *ja* but you have no idea how this change of heart is supposed to suddenly sweep down on hundreds of people?"

Her eyes and lips smiled. "The Christmas spirit maybe?" She kissed him on the cheek. "It's not my problem. Or yours. It's God's." She linked her arm through one of his. "You should drive us home now, my husband."

$\sim\infty\sim$

Rebecca was standing at the door with her hands on her hips as the buggy pulled into the yard.

"You two have been gone a long time," she said. "I was worried."

Naomi climbed down from the buggy. "Worried about what?"

Rebecca studied her friend's face. A smile slipped over her mouth. "Oh, worried you might have been fighting. But now that I see you, I realize that's not the case."

"What do you mean?"

"Someone has been kissing," Rebecca whispered.

Red sprang onto Naomi's cheeks, and Rebecca's smile grew. "This is a good thing, *ja*? After all, he is your husband and he's been gone a long time. When you left the house you were ice. You come back and you have thawed. So I praise the Lord. That's one prayer answered, and answered very quickly for such a difficult matter. Now I have high hopes all the other prayers I'm praying will be answered just as swiftly."

# Four

A fresh snowfall came in the door with Bishop Fischer and the ministers Sunday afternoon. Naomi and Rebecca helped them hang their coats and hats on pegs and then served them coffee as they sat by the woodstove in the parlor. Micah joined them. The two women went into the kitchen, leaving the men to their talk.

"Not so hot as the desert, eh?" asked the bishop, holding his hands toward the stove and rubbing them.

Micah smiled. "Summer days and summer nights are both warm in Kandahar, it's true. But nights in Kabul are cooler."

"I suppose it didn't make any difference to you with the work you did."

"No, sir. You go to the sick and wounded no matter what the weather conditions are or how hot the temperature is. The same way you would go to someone in the church if they were hurt or ill, Bishop Fischer."

"Well. It's not the same thing, Micah."

"Why not, sir?"

"I would go because it is a bishop's duty, a calling from God."

"I did it for the same reason."

The bishop breathed out noisily. "Micah—"

Micah looked at the bishop over the rim of his coffee cup. "If one of your draught horses was injured on Sunday, would you bring in the vet?"

"No, no, not if it wasn't serious. It could wait for Monday."

"What if it was life threatening?"

The bishop tugged at his untrimmed gray beard with his thick fingers. "I see where you're going with this, young man. Still, it's not the same. We are in a Christian environment here. A war zone is not a holy place."

"Just suppose, God forbid, two drug gangs had a fight along one of our roads here, in front of several of our farms."

"Nonsense." Minister Yoder, bald, spectacled, with a long black beard and huge arms folded across his chest, glared at Micah.

"Suppose one car was chasing another, shots were fired, a car crashed, more gunfire—a gang war right in the middle of our Amish community. Then one car speeds away and leaves behind a burning wreck and bodies in the ditch."

"We call the police," growled Minister Yoder. "And the ambulance."

"Of course. But it will take them some time to get here. What will you do until then?"

"Pray."

"Yes, Minister, pray, but meanwhile men are bleeding to death. These are not holy men, not churchmen, not Amish men, but they are men made in the image of God. What will you do?"

"You and your trick questions," Minister Yoder rumbled. "Suppose, suppose. We do not live in the world of suppose, suppose. Such a thing would never happen here."

Micah sipped at his coffee. "Jesus lived in the world of suppose, suppose."

"What?"

"All his stories. All his parables. The events never happened. But he told the stories so he could get people to think about what they believed, about what they would do. He told them to get people to think about what they *should* do. Just as I'm doing now."

"He was the Lord Jesus Christ and you are not!"

Micah set down his coffee cup. "Who is your neighbor, Minister Yoder?"

The door to the parlor was closed, but Naomi and Rebecca could hear the men's voices as the two women sat at the kitchen table and sewed up the tears in Luke's clothing.

Rebecca shook her head and smiled. "They will never out argue Micah."

Naomi had stopped using her needle, listening for a response. But the parlor was silent until the bishop spoke again.

"I see where you're going with this. Yes, we would care for them just as you cared for men on the battlefield. The difference is, you went looking for trouble but we deal with what the Lord brings across our path, no more than that."

Naomi heard Micah's reply. "Jesus went looking for trouble."

"Nonsense." Minister Yoder again.

"He could have stayed in Nazareth. Made people come to him. But he didn't. He went to them. Even to the war zone."

"What war zone is this?" the bishop asked.

"Jerusalem. Where he knew they wanted to kill him. But he went anyway. Healed the sick. Cured the lame. Made the blind see. Closed up wounds. Stopped the bleeding. Dealt with head injuries and eye injuries and back injuries. He was a divine medic. A holy army surgeon."

"He was no medic or surgeon, young man. He did not heal men so they could fight again and take other men's lives."

"But he did. Don't you think the Roman centurion fought? Don't you think his servant helped him prepare for battle? Yet Jesus healed the servant."

Silence.

Micah's voice again. "Jesus didn't ask many questions. If a

person had faith, that was enough. Do we know what every man or woman was like before they came to Jesus for help? Were they all pure? Were they all good? And what happened after they were healed? Did they make mistakes and errors in judgment, did they curse or lie or steal or hurt others? Or were they perfect for the rest of their lives?"

More silence.

"The war with the Romans came thirty or forty years after Jesus was crucified. Some of the men he healed, especially the young, would have taken up arms against the Roman occupation. They would have fought and killed and been killed. Yet Jesus healed them anyway. He healed everyone, knowing that some of them might do harm with their new lives, might rob, murder, or blaspheme. He healed men who worked for soldiers and men who would become soldiers.

"I don't know what all the men and women I bandaged and gave blood transfusions and saved did with their new lives. *Ja*, some went back into combat. But others went home. What sort of people are they now? Good, kind, gracious, forgiving? Petty, cruel, bitter, harsh? I have no idea. That's in God's hands. I only tried to do what Jesus did—go and find the hurt and wounded and heal them, whoever they were and wherever they were. I wanted to be like him in Afghanistan. Just like him."

Naomi closed her eyes and bent her head.

*But he is right. Everything he says is right. His words are much stronger than they were a year ago. He has thought about this. He has prayed about this. They must agree with him.*

"You have a lot to say, don't you?" Minister Yoder's voice was deep. "A lot to say and you think you are Jesus now. You go to the desert and come back Jesus, hm? But you are only a man, a sinner, and your words are worthless. You took your vows, you were baptized, and you knew when you joined the army—yes, even as a medic—that you were breaking the *Ordnung*. All this fancy talk of yours is pointless. Either you repent or you don't. It is as straight-forward as that."

"It seems to me you have meant well." The bishop said more softly. "You did nothing in malice or with deceit. But we do not go to war, not even to heal, no, not even for that. Will you lay this down before the Lord? Will you confess your disobedience?"

The two women couldn't hear Micah's response.

"Very well. So the *bann* will go into effect once again at the end of the day, at the stroke of twelve. You know all that you must not do while this is in force. To everything else, I add this—you will do none of your medical work among us, all that you learned at the military base here in America, all you learned in Afghanistan, all the army taught you…no, none of it you will practice. Do you understand?"

"I do understand, *ja*."

"So we pray and leave you with your soul and your conscience in the hands of the Lord."

It was quiet for five minutes though both women could hear murmuring as the men prayed. Then the parlor door opened, and the ministers and Bishop Fischer filed out. They nodded to Naomi and Rebecca, put on their coats and hats, and left, snow swirling thicker and faster over their shoulders and backs. The wheels creaked and the horses snorted as their hooves chopped the ice and frozen mud. They were gone. Rebecca shut the door tightly.

"It's almost dark," she said.

Naomi was standing and looking at her husband, who had emerged quietly from the parlor.

"My coffee got cold." He held up his cup. "I talked too much and didn't drink enough. The talking part won't be an issue for a few months or years now that the *bann* is in force again."

"You reasoned well," said his sister.

"Not well enough. I thought I had a better approach than a year ago, better ideas, better Scriptures…but apparently not."

"It *was* better, brother."

"Was it? It swayed no one."

Naomi came and took the cup from his hand. "It swayed me."

He looked at her sharply. "What?"

"What you said was right. I know it. I couldn't refute your arguments. Neither could they. So they ran and hid behind the *Ordnung*. You broke their rules, and that's all that matters to them. Should the *Ordnung* be changed? *Ja.* Will they change it? No." She smiled. "At least, not yet."

Half of his mouth curved upward. "You think you can get someone like Minister Yoder to change the *Ordnung*? You think you can get someone like Minister Yoder to change his mind?"

"It's not necessary to change Minister Yoder. It's only necessary to change the bishop. If he says *ja*, it is *ja*. If he says *nein*, it is *nein*."

"And you think that will be easy?"

"I didn't say it would be easy." She grasped his hand and led him to the table. "Sit. I'll pour you the coffee you never enjoyed because you were too busy preaching your sermon."

"A sermon that fell on deaf ears."

She pinched his ear. "Am I deaf?"

"Hey! That hurt."

"So remember who heard you. I should be a big enough convert for you for the moment."

"Then you're saying you understand?"

Naomi emptied his cold coffee in the sink. "No, I'm not saying I understand. Just that I believe your argument is sound. And scriptural. But do I understand? You could have accomplished the same thing by joining an EMS team here in Pennsylvania." She poured fresh coffee from a pot on the stove and set his cup down in front of him. "They save lives too. But not in a war zone."

"So you don't understand." Micah stared into the dark coffee, wrapping his hands around the mug. "You don't understand why it had to be Afghanistan. Neither of you do."

Rebecca mussed his hair. "As we like to say in this house, that's God's problem. He put the call in your heart. So if he wants to, he can explain the call to us. Or not."

Naomi sat down with her own coffee. "That goes for the bishop too. You could argue till you're blue in the face and get nowhere. God has to show him."

"I could argue with Yoder."

"Yoder, well, with Yoder your face would be purple."

The three of them laughed. Rebecca brought matches from a pocket in her dress and lit the candle on the table. Then she walked around the room, lighting other candles and lanterns.

"I must go check on Luke." Naomi patted Micah's hand. "He was sleeping soundly through all that business with the leadership."

"No. I'm already on my way up." Rebecca was carrying a lantern in one hand and coffee in the other as she climbed the staircase. "You two need to talk. In a few hours you'll be like Trappists as far as speaking with one another is concerned."

"Thank you, Becca." Naomi put a hand over both of Micah's as he held the hot cup of coffee. "Just because I don't understand now doesn't mean I won't understand tomorrow."

"What will it take, I wonder?"

"Being there. But that will never happen. Naomi Bachman shall never set foot in Kandahar or Kabul. Micah Bachman did, yes, for that was his call. It is not mine."

"If it takes being there to touch your heart, your heart will never be touched."

"Well, you know the saying—what's impossible with us is a short day's work with God."

The small smile she had missed for more than a year came over his lips. "I'll miss your voice, Omi, once the *bann* goes into effect again."

"You will hear my voice every day."

"But not directed to me."

She squeezed his hands. "The *bann* will not last forever."

"You said it the other day—how do we know? One day is as a thousand years to God."

"The Lord will do something. I don't know what. But our story isn't going to end in silence with you under a *bann* because you saved dying men's lives."

He brought her hand to his lips and kissed it. "I love your faith."

"My faith isn't faith in myself or my abilities, Micah."

"I know that. But I love it just the same. Just as I love you."

Her warmest smile came to her face. "A woman doesn't need words to tell her man she loves him. There's no *bann* against looking at me. I think you like to look at me."

"Oh, *ja*."

"So look into my eyes every morning, every afternoon, every evening. Look as long as you like. You will hear everything you need to hear right there."

His small smile became a large smile. "I like the sound of that."

"I'll stop whatever I'm doing, I don't care what it is. Just stand before me, and I will face you and you may gaze as long as you wish." She winked. "So long as the favor is returned and I may gaze at your handsome face whenever the notion strikes me."

"That shouldn't be too hard a favor to grant. But suppose I never break off my gaze? Suppose I get lost in those dreamy eyes of yours and never walk away?"

"Suppose, suppose. We do not live in the land of suppose, suppose, Micah Bachman."

"I do. All people of faith do."

"*Ja*." She stood up, slender and dark, a burning in her eyes. "So do I." Standing over him, she placed one strong hand at the back of his neck, tilted his face toward her own, and bent down to kiss him. Strands of her hair fell over his closed eyes and his cheeks. Then all her dark hair seemed to be covering him, and he took in its spicy perfume. He reached up and pulled her into his lap. Her prayer *kapp* was gone, and so were her pins. The avalanche of sweet blackness overwhelmed him.

"I love you, Micah," she murmured as they kissed. "I ached for you while you were gone. I was literally in pain. No one will take you from me again. No army, no *bann*, no bishop. Every day look at me. Every day gaze at me like you gaze on a field of red poppies or a herd of fine horses grazing in the tall grass. I will not disappoint you. Each morning my hair will be washed just for you. My face scrubbed and fresh. My dress smoothed of wrinkles. Did they say I couldn't smile at you? I will smile as if you were the sun on my face and the blue sky of summer in my eyes. I will smile as if you were the moonlight and stars of August. No one will stop me from loving you. I don't need German or English words. It's as the Scriptures themselves say, my speech will fill your ears even if there is no sound."

He placed his head on her chest. She cradled him and whispered, "The heavens tell us of the glory of God. Day after day, night after night. They speak without the slightest sound, without the tiniest word. You can't hear a voice. Yet what they say goes out into all the earth, the words carry to the ends of the world. So it is for you and me, Micah Bachman. My language will be the love I bear for you, a love I'll bear until the day I die. I don't need syllables and vowels. Only my smile, only my eyes, only my soul."

# Five

But things did not go as smoothly as Naomi had hoped.

Every morning she dressed as neatly as if she were a new bride and homemaker. She washed her face and hands, brushed out her hair till it gleamed, twisted it back into a perfect bun, placed her prayer *kapp* on her head, and joined Rebecca in a kitchen lit by lanterns, where they prepared the breakfasts Micah enjoyed the most. If Micah's gaze rested on her, she let it and did not walk away. If his eyes found hers, she did not look down or to the side, but looked right back with all the feeling for him she had locked inside her.

"Your love for my brother is obvious," Rebecca said quietly as she placed a pitcher of cream back in the icebox.

"I'm glad," replied Naomi. "He's my husband. That's how it should be."

"I wonder what Minister Yoder would have to say about the way you and Micah look at one another when you are under the *bann*?"

"So now our eyes are under the *Ordnung* too? We can't talk to each other, and now we can't look at each other either?"

"Words are spoken with the eyes," said Rebecca.

"*Ja?*" Naomi put away a loaf of bread. "And what do they say?"

"I've already told you."

"So when love is banned from our Amish community, please be the first to tell me so that I may pack my bags."

"I didn't mean to censure you. But others see how you look at him when they visit us. They could complain to the bishop and make matters worse for you. They could demand Micah leave the house or community."

Rebecca's words bothered Naomi. But it wasn't just the words that bothered her. She found that whenever she met Micah in the house or in the yard and their eyes found one another and the love for him lit every part of her body, not being able to hold him or kiss him or speak to him became harder and harder to bear. And making herself perfect for him, cooking his favorite food, and letting him hold his gaze on her just made matters worse. Day after day she grew more and more miserable and began to avoid Micah whenever she could.

"So love has taken a strange twist," remarked Rebecca as they sewed by the front window that looked out on the fields and the main road.

Naomi's eyes snapped with a sudden burst of light. "If it has taken a twist, it's the *Ordnung* that has twisted it. I haven't seen my husband for a year—he could have been killed!—and now we're in the same house together and we can't talk, we can't touch. I sleep alone while he makes his bed among worn-out rockers and broken cuckoo clocks. I think I'm going to lose my mind."

"Pray. Seek God."

"Pray for what? For Micah to change his mind? Or the bishop and the ministers?"

"Both."

"Ha. Both. *Gut.* That's easy enough."

"For God it is."

"*Ja*, sure, for God. But I'm the one who's a widow. There's no difference between myself and Deborah Lantz. She lost her husband to a barn fire. I lost mine to the war and the *Ordnung*."

"He's still alive. You see him every day."

Naomi dropped her sewing on the table. "He might as well be dead. What good does seeing him every day do? We're like ghosts to each other. I thought the smiles and the warmth would be enough, but I was wrong. It's torture. It was easier to bear when I couldn't see him at all."

Rebecca also put her sewing aside. "Thank God for what you have."

"That's easy for you to say." Naomi put a hand over her eyes. She sighed. "I'm sorry, Rebecca. Of course, it isn't. I've had many griefs, but so have you. You've also lost grandparents and others you loved in your lifetime."

"But not my God. Not my faith. And neither have you."

"I seem to be on the verge some days. He asks too much of me."

"He will give you the grace you need to handle it."

"*Ja*? When?"

"I don't know when. I don't know how. But that's his problem to deal with. Not yours or mine."

Naomi dropped her hand from red and puffy eyes. "And so what's my problem to deal with then?"

"To not lose hope."

"Hope. *Ja*, well, hope is good. But I see no way out of this. It's the most snarled-up ball of yarn I've ever laid eyes on. I'm at a loss. I feel trapped."

Rebecca put a hand on her arm. "I don't want to come across as though I'm judging you and Micah. Truly, I'm on your side. The Lord who knows my heart can tell you I wish you to be in each other's arms again and Micah to be welcomed back into the Amish community. Perhaps I'm too forthright with my tongue. Pardon me for that. But I'm not against you. I would rather the *Ordnung* changed its position than my brother changed his. I don't believe there's a great chance of that. Yet as I say, it's God's problem. If it's true he sent Micah to war to be a healer in the name of Christ, then yes, it's completely and utterly his problem. Ours is to remain steadfast and anchored in him."

Naomi stared out the window as snow began to fall and wind began to swirl it in tight circles. "I wish my mother were here. I wish I could speak with her."

Rebecca squeezed her arm. "You can."

"What do you mean?"

"She kept a book. You always told me about her book."

A small smile came to Naomi's face. "*Das Buch von Wunder.*" *Her book of wonders.*

"Didn't she leave messages in it for you to read?"

"*Ja, ja.* Not just me. Papa. Luke. Ruth. It was her way."

"She spoke to God in it, didn't she?"

"*Ja.* Sometimes she asked us to read those conversations, those prayers. Other times no, she sealed those pages from us if she put the book in our hands."

Rebecca interlaced her fingers with Naomi's. "Do you know where this book is?"

Naomi's eyebrows came together. "Why, I haven't thought about it. No. Somewhere in their room, I suppose. I can't go in there. I can't bear to. Not yet."

"*Ja.* I know. But I have been in there. When I cleaned your parents' room I saw the book. It was impossible not to notice. It was lying open on the table by the window. Your mother—" Rebecca paused and took a breath, glancing out at the snowfall. "She had been writing in it that morning before she climbed into the buggy."

"What?"

"I read very little of it. Only enough to make note of the date. Then I closed it and put it away."

"And you didn't say anything?"

Rebecca continued to watch the snow. "I felt you had enough pain to deal with. But now perhaps you should sit down and read what she wrote her final morning on earth."

"The way you put it, I'm almost afraid to."

"Don't be afraid. She was your mother. She loved you."

"Was…was what she wrote addressed to me?"

Rebecca nodded. "*Ja*."

Naomi slipped her fingers from Rebecca's and slowly got to her feet. "Where will I…where will I find the book?"

"Under her pillow." Rebecca picked up her sewing again. "I will pray for you, Naomi."

"*Danke*."

"I'll be here by the window when you've finished, Naomi. If you wish to talk."

Naomi crossed the house to the staircase. She stared up the flight of steps to the second floor.

*Lord, I don't want to go into that room. I will just cry my eyes out once I open the door and see their bed and the clothes still hanging in their closet. I cannot do it. Every day you ask too much of me.*

She climbed the stairs as if it hurt her to move each leg. At the top she waited again. She was tempted to look in on Luke, but she had just taken a peek an hour before. Biting her lip, she walked along the hall to the door with the well-worn brass knob. Resting her hand on it, she closed her eyes, twisted it, and opened the door. The air was cool. Scents of the room rushed over her like a breeze from an open window.

*Mama's hand cream she used to get rid of the dryness. Papa's shaving soap to keep his upper lip clear. The dried flowers Mama kept in a jar.*

She opened her eyes. The snow was falling faster and thicker and coating the windows. She entered the room and closed the door behind her, leaning with her back against it a moment. She felt as if both her parents would be sitting on their sides of the bed that night and talking as they always had. Nothing looked out of place. Rebecca had kept the room tidy. It was as though her mother had just swept the floor and wiped down the furniture with a damp cloth.

"Blessings on this place," she whispered. "Blessings on your souls in the Lord Jesus Christ."

She went to the bed and gently turned her mother's pillow over. The book was there as Rebecca had said. She lifted it up. It was bound in the dark brown leather her father had tanned himself. Sitting on the bed she pressed her lips to it and smelled the thick leather and the cream from her mother's hands. She was careful as she opened it, for she remembered that several old flowers were pressed between its pages.

## Six

The book fell open to the middle, and a dried red rose fell into her lap.

Naomi glanced at the fine, almost spidery writing of her mother's fountain pen. She had never been shown these pages. They were prayers for each of the children. She read the ones for her sister and for Luke. Putting the book down, she looked at the snowfall again, bracing herself. Then she read the prayers her mother had written for her.

> For Naomi, Lord, you must find a man stronger than her. She is sweet, and I've always thought of her as my little muffin. But somehow into my recipe fell all sorts of scraps of iron from my husband's workshop. She is a blue sky one moment and a tempest the next. Calm her spirit, yes, but do not remove it. I love my spirited mare. No, for her, I ask you, far more so than I do for Ruth, that you gift her with a man whose spirit matches

*hers, or he will never do and she will quickly be bored with him.*

"Oh, Mama." Naomi laughed as tears moved down from her eyes. "This is five years ago. Is that truly how you thought of me when I was so young?"

*So now the Bachman's boy Micah brings her home in his buggy. I don't know what to think. Something about him strikes me wrong. My muffin is taken with his looks, but only you know the look of his heart. Direct her steps. Give her father and me wisdom in this matter.*

"What?" Naomi held the book tightly in her hands, and the tears stopped. "What was wrong with Micah? Oh…you always liked the Fischer boys. Please, Mama."

*I have no argument against their marriage. But I know why I've felt some concern. Micah has a mind of his own. His spirit is very free, much freer than my muffin's. I don't know what will come of this. I don't sense any objection from you in my heart. And I don't read any objection from you in your Word. So we go ahead and put every day of Micah's and Naomi's in your good hands.*

"Mama, you were very happy on our wedding day. You loved the clock he gave me for a wedding present. The little man announcing the hour by bringing the workhorse out of the barn, *ja*? So but now it is broken."

*I knew this. I knew this in my soul. What Amish man up and joins the army and says he must bind the wounds of the soldiers who fall in battle? Who has ever heard of such a thing among the Amish? He knows he will be shunned. He knows it will break my Naomi's heart. I knew he had this spirit in him. What will you do now, my Lord? Where are you taking us?*

There were no more prayers for Naomi. She turned to the back of the book. A dozen blank pages. She ran her fingers over their smooth whiteness. Then she forced herself to look at the last writing her mother had done.

*Naomi,*

*I will share this with you in the evening. Let me think on it a while during the trip to town. But I think it is good. I think it is from God.*

*Micah will come back to you. I'm certain of it. He won't die. He will not forget his vows to you. So you must not forget your vows to him. Ja, of course, he has forgotten his vows to his people, to his church, but not, I think, to his God or to his bride. So even if others don't welcome his return, you must.*

*The bishop may not let you embrace him with your arms. But you must embrace him with your prayers. That's how you will show him your love.*

*There is more to Micah than I thought. The more I pray, the more I'm convinced of it. I don't say he hasn't made mistakes or been rash. But even while he's shunned, it will be up to you, up to all of us in this family he has married into, to surround him with the love of God. Without words, without touch. All around him we are to place the love of God.*

*I will give this to you to read tonight if it still sits well with me. Then we shall talk about it. Then we shall pray.*

*My love, Mama*

The tears were sparks on her face, burning against her skin.

She got up from the bed, put the rose back inside the pages of the book, tucked the book back under the pillow, and left the room, closing the door softly. Standing in the hall, she heard the sound of an axe from outside the house. She went to a small window and looked out and saw Micah in a toque and parka chopping firewood, snow whirling around him.

*How cold you must be. Cold and alone.*

Naomi made up her mind, wiped her cheeks with the back of her hand, and marched to a nearby closet. Broom and dustpan in hand, she opened Micah's bedroom door. She was surprised to find his bed neatly made, all the items to be repaired arranged from small to large against the far wall, and everything exactly as it should be in every part of the room. It even looked as if the hard-wood floor had been swept.

"Well, twice can't hurt, soldier," she muttered and set about sweeping the room and under the bed and wiping a cloth over everything. She left the door open so she could hear the sound of the axe. As she listened, she prayed for Micah as her mother had wanted her to.

*Rrrrrrrrrrrrmmmmmmm.*

"What is that?"

For a moment she thought it was a motorcycle. Then she thought it was a chainsaw and groaned. *Oh, Micah, don't make matters worse by using power tools.*

She went out into the hall and glanced out the window, half expecting to see her husband using a gas generator to run a saw. Micah had laid aside his axe, but not in order to wield a power tool. He was listening to a boy who was straddling a red motorbike. She couldn't see who the boy was because he had his back to her.

*Doesn't he know it is forbidden to speak with Micah?*

Micah folded his arms over his chest, nodded his head once or twice, and smiled, but he didn't respond in any other way.

*Thank goodness you have kept your head. The boy cannot go home and tell his parents that Micah Bachman talked to him.*

Naomi closed the door to Micah's room, returned the broom and dustpan to the hall closet, opened the door to Luke's bedroom a crack and found he was still napping, and then came quickly down the stairs to where Rebecca was sewing.

"There's a boy on a motorbike talking to Micah," she said. "Can you believe that?"

"Oh, it's Minister Yoder's son, Timothy." Rebecca glanced up, her face sharp. "Micah isn't holding a conversation with him, I hope."

"No, no, just listening."

"Well, that boy likes to hear his own voice, so it doesn't matter if Micah responds or not."

"But since when can Minister Yoder's son do this? A motorbike? Talking to a person who's banned from the church? It's not his *rumspringa*, not so soon."

"It *is* his *rumspringa*. For more than a week now. Your mind has been elsewhere."

"So the minister buys his son a motorbike?"

Rebecca lifted one shoulder in a shrug. "If he promises to drive it around here, he gets the bike. That's the minister's way of having his son where he can keep his eyes on him."

"So *rumspringa* and motorbikes are okay, but healing wounded soldiers in Afghanistan is a sin?"

"The minister's boy has not taken his vows. He hasn't broken faith with the Amish people. Micah did take his vows. He did break faith with the Amish people. That's how they see it."

"And the people are all right with this noisy bike?"

Rebecca shrugged again. "They were all right a few years ago when Bishop Fischer let his boy drive that old blue pickup for six months. The church considers it better than wild parties and looks the other way."

"And how do we know there aren't wild parties too?"

"There's no gossip about such parties. Not yet. The church is willing to put up with the bike."

Timothy roared past the house, and they watched him spray snow and dirt on his way to the main road.

A minute later Micah came into the house, stamping his boots, removing them, and hanging up his coat. He was holding a slender package under one arm as he looked toward Naomi. She dropped her eyes, and he went up the stairs to his room.

"Did you read your mother's book?" asked Rebecca.

"*Ja.*"

"And so?"

"And so she wants me to pray for him and believe the best of him and support him as a wife should support a husband even though there is a *bann*."

"But she didn't know Micah would come home."

"She was certain God would bring him back. And she was certain he would come to me and want our marriage to continue. She was insistent I be close to him once more regardless of what he had done or what punishment the church inflicted on him."

Rebecca gave a little smile. "Such a good woman, your mother."

"*Ja.*" Naomi picked up her sewing and put it down again. "But I still don't see how this will work. It's too hard to be apart from him. It's too hard to see him and not be able to hold him. My mother wished me to love him from afar. *Ja*, when he was in Afghanistan and now when he's only a few feet away and might as well still be in Afghanistan."

"Something will work out."

"I don't see how."

"It is not up to you to see how. Only to walk by faith and not by sight." Rebecca took Naomi's hand. "Let me pray for you."

Rebecca prayed a long time. They heard Micah come down the staircase and go back outside while their heads were bent. After the prayer they got up and saw a rocking chair in the kitchen.

Naomi's fingers went to her mouth. "That's my mother's. It broke a week before her death. The left rocker had split."

They got up and examined it.

"It has a new rocker now." Rebecca bent down. "You would hardly know it's new. The stain matches the rest of the chair perfectly."

"He does very good work."

Rebecca stood up and smiled. "You should sit and rock."

"No." Naomi shook her head. "I'm not sitting in that chair."

"Why not?"

"No." Naomi went to the icebox. "It's time to start supper."

They cooked a pot of cabbage soup and took a bowl of it up to Luke. Working together, they managed to get him into his chair, but half the soup was wasted as they tried to feed it to him. When they came back down, Micah was serving himself from the pot. He barely glanced at the two of them as he walked into the parlor and shut the door. Rebecca and Naomi sat down at the kitchen table, prayed, and began to eat. Neither of them spoke.

"We're as silent as Luke and Micah," murmured Rebecca.

"We've said everything there is to say for the day."

"Soon it will be one great big quiet house."

"That's not so bad sometimes, is it?" asked Naomi.

"No, not so bad. Sometimes."

That night Naomi lay in her bed in the dark and thought about Micah lying in his bed in the dark at the end of the hall. She prayed for him. She prayed for Luke. She prayed for Rebecca. Then she came back and prayed for Micah again.

*What will you do for him, Lord? What will you do for our marriage? And how long will you take to do it?*

God seemed as silent to her as the house. She rolled over on her side and tried to sleep.

# Seven

Three letters arrived the day before Thanksgiving. One was an early Christmas card. All were addressed to her. All three had something to say about her husband, Sergeant Micah Bachman, medic, United States Army. She read each one, startled at the information they contained, and at first she had no thought of sharing any of them.

*What is this you're bringing into my life now, Lord? What prayer do these cards and letters answer?*

Micah stayed with Luke during the Thanksgiving worship held at Bishop Fischer's home. It was followed by a meal, so Naomi and Rebecca were gone for several hours. Once they returned, Micah smiled, put on his coat and hat, and left in silence. Naomi watched him drive a buggy out to the main road and head in the direction of Lancaster. Four hours later he returned with the same sort of smile and silence in which he had left.

"I can't get used to this," Naomi told Rebecca. "All this quiet."

"The whole year he was gone you couldn't talk to him."

"So now I'm to be thankful for another such year?"

Rebecca put a hand on Naomi's shoulder. "Take it to God."

"Where else should I take it?" She folded her arms over her chest. "I told you. It was easier when he was away. Out of sight, out of mind, as the *Englisch* say. But now I see him every day and I can't speak a word, I can't hold him, I can't lie with him as God ordained a woman should lie with her husband. It's cruel."

"In time this will be resolved."

"Whose time? Mine? God's? If it were in my time it would have been settled weeks ago. The leadership knew they could not in good faith refute Micah's arguments for following Christ's leading to the battlefield. No, not when he went there to save human life. So they ran and crouched behind the *Ordnung*. If it is to be in God's time, it could be a thousand years from today."

"It won't be a thousand years, Naomi."

"It could be never."

◦◦◦

The week after Thanksgiving, there were three more cards and two letters. Rebecca saw them but said nothing. One card brought Naomi to tears as she sat reading it at the kitchen table. Unable to keep her emotions in check, she turned in her chair and practically cried out to her friend, "Oh, Rebecca, come here. Please, come and sit with me. I must read you this note from a woman in Ohio."

Rebecca left off kneading the dough for the week's bread, wiped her hands on a towel, and came to the table, taking a seat across from Naomi, who kept brushing at her eyes with one hand. In the other she held a Christmas card of baby Jesus in a manger.

"This woman's husband was in Afghanistan. He was out in front of his platoon and was shot by the enemy. The whole platoon was caught in an ambush. They couldn't go forward or backward. Only crouch down and shoot back. No one was able to go to rescue her wounded husband. The shooting was too great. No one would go to her husband. Only Micah."

She tried to read the card but was unable to speak. Rebecca reached over and gently took it from her fingers.

As the company medic, your husband had already accepted the fact that he must go wherever the wounded were. He understood that often enough it would be where enemy fire was heaviest and the risk of being shot the greatest. So he went after my Sam when no one else would or could. Sam tells me bullets were kicking up sand and stone all around him. The next thing he knew he was being dragged behind a rock at least a hundred feet away. He has no idea why he did not get hit again or why your husband did not get killed. Sgt. Micah Bachman got Sam's bleeding under control, gave him morphine, prayed with him, and once air support had cleared the enemy out, carried Sam to safety. We have a Christmas this year with Sam surrounded by his children because your husband risked his life to save him. Greater love hath no man than this. How privileged you are to have Micah Bachman as your husband. From the bottom of my heart, from all his sons and daughters, thank you and God bless you both.

Rebecca closed the card and laid it on the table. "I see," was all she was able to get out. She bowed her head, and Naomi could see the struggle in her face. Eyes damp, she finally looked up again. "I wonder that the card came to you and not to him or to both of you."

"A woman explained that in a letter last week. Micah had said that while he was in the field any letters or notes should be addressed to his wife in Pennsylvania. I suppose that was in case he should…" She couldn't finish.

Rebecca took Naomi by the hand. "God is good. *Ja*, Micah has returned to us. And his good works for these men—his good works for God—have not been forgotten by these people. They thought to write."

Naomi nodded.

"Why now, though? Why all at once?" Rebecca asked.

"A number were readdressed. Despite what Micah told people, some went to his unit. Then, of course, it's Thanksgiving and Christmas, isn't it? The *Englisch* set great store by Thanksgiving and Christmas."

"How many of these do you have now?"

"I don't know. Eight or nine, I think. Each one I open blesses me. And each one stings."

Rebecca reached over and put her hand on Naomi's arm. "Perhaps there won't be any more. Maybe this is all there is."

"Maybe."

But the letters and cards continued to come. Two or three a week. Naomi read each one and then shared with Rebecca, who took to reading them out loud when Micah was in the house. He might be eating alone in the parlor. Or upstairs with Luke, the bedroom door open. Or just coming in the door from tending to the cattle. But she read them with the intent he hear each and every word. Sometimes, if he was nearby, he might stand and listen. Other times he quietly walked away or closed the parlor or bedroom door.

One day a letter came that changed everything for Naomi. In it a young soldier's mother talked about her son's death in battle. How Micah had done everything in his power to save his life. How other soldiers in the unit had told her he wept when her son died in his arms and how he had insisted on carrying her boy's body back behind their lines, half a mile in the desert heat. As if that weren't enough, two months later Micah had run through a hail of bullets and rocket fire to save her nephew from a burning helicopter—her nephew and seven others, including three women soldiers. Two other medics had worked with him, one of whom had been killed rescuing the pilot. Her nephew was joining them for Christmas in Texas. She had put off writing long enough, she said.

The enduring image she had was of her young son, in his death, being held and carried in the arms of Naomi's husband with as much love and strength as if he were the boy's own father. Micah's battledress had been soaked in blood, the other men had told her. But he would not take it off.

> I thank God that someone loved my son as much in death as I loved him in life. I thank God that when he died, the Lord made sure someone would be there who would treat him with gentleness and respect. I thank God that is the manner in which my son left the earth, in a brave man's arms.

Her cheeks wet, Naomi went to the parlor where Micah sat eating soup alone and in silence. She read the letter out loud. Then she stared at him.

"Is it true, Micah Bachman?"

Rebecca came into the parlor. "Hush, Naomi. You are breaking the *Ordnung*."

"I don't care. He must answer me this question."

"If they find out they will place you under the *bann* as well."

"How will they find out? Will you tell them?"

"Of course not."

"It's understood I may speak with him if it's an emergency."

Rebecca glanced from Naomi's face to the letter in her hand. "This is not an emergency."

"Oh, *ja*, it is." She didn't take her eyes off Micah. "Did you not hear me read it, Rebecca?"

"I was feeding Luke."

Naomi handed her the sheet of paper, still staring at her husband. She waited until Rebecca had finished. Her friend drew in a deep breath and placed a hand over her heart.

"My brother," was all she said.

Naomi's eyes were black flames. "I'm not leaving this room

until you answer me, Sergeant Micah Bachman. Is this letter true? Does she exaggerate or is what she tells me exactly what happened?"

Micah looked back at her, silent. Finally he nodded.

Naomi went on. "And where is the uniform you wore that day? Do you still have it?"

Micah nodded again.

"Tell me the truth—did you ever wash it? Did you ever wash out that young boy's blood?"

He hesitated, not responding for several long seconds. Then he shook his head.

Naomi flew from the room and snatched her winter coat off a peg by the front door.

"Where are you going?" asked Rebecca, running after her. "Don't do anything rash."

Naomi wrapped a black scarf about her neck with swift movements. "I'm going to Bishop Fischer."

"Bishop Fischer? What's your business with him?"

Naomi took the letter from Rebecca's hand. "This letter is my business." She gazed almost wildly at her friend and then shifted her eyes to a cupboard over one of the counters. She marched across the kitchen and took down a packet of letters tied with a red ribbon. "And these as well."

Micah had already used Maria and the buggy that morning and had not yet unharnessed the mare. Naomi sprang into the driver's seat and snapped the reins. Maria pulled out of the farmyard at a fast trot. Rebecca stood at the window and watched Naomi drive onto the main road.

She was at the bishop's house in ten minutes.

"Naomi," the bishop greeted her as he opened the door. "Good day. What brings you out on such a frosty morning?"

Naomi's smile was short and sweet. "Good day, Bishop Fischer. I'm sorry to come by just before lunch."

"No, no, Mary tells me it will be another forty-five minutes. Come, come, let me help you with your coat."

Naomi didn't remove her coat. "I need you to read these." She thrust the packet of letters at him. "It's important."

"Why, what's in them?"

"I can't explain."

He took the packet. "Now? You wish me to look at them here and now?"

"Please. You need only read a few."

He looked at the dark fire in her eyes. "Very well, very well. Have a seat."

She sat in the offered seat as he untied the ribbon and put it in his pocket and then slipped on his reading glasses. He opened a Christmas card and read it quickly. His face gave no sign of how it affected him. He opened a second card. Again his features remained just as they had been when he first took the packet from her. Selecting a letter, he took it from its envelope and unfolded it. As he read he suddenly lowered himself into a chair, his eyes still on the words handwritten across the paper. Then he folded it back up and returned it to its envelope and opened another card, one with a Thanksgiving pumpkin on it. Finishing it, he tapped the card against his knee and looked up at her, glasses still on his face.

"So. How long has this been going on?"

"They began to come just before Thanksgiving Day."

"And more came even today?"

"*Ja*. This one." She offered him the letter from the mother of the boy who had died in Micah's arms and whose body Micah had carried. This time she saw a reaction in the bishop's face. It seemed to her he read the letter twice. Then he looked off into the front room and through a window to the fields of snow outside.

"*Ja, ja*," he murmured. "God's ways are strange. They are not our ways. It's up to us to learn from him and not the other way around." He looked at her. "These must touch your heart, *dochter*."

"Yes, they touch me deeply. As I hoped they would you."

He sighed and looked out the window again. "They do touch me, child. But you must understand—the *Ordnung* is the *Ordnung*. It has been thus with our people for hundreds of years as they followed God."

"Sometimes the *Ordnung* changes."

"Not often, *dochter*."

"But sometimes. You even told me so once when I was a child. You permitted rubber tires on our buggies because they don't jar the older people so much on the long drives."

"*Ja, ja*, but buggy wheels are one thing. What you are asking is much bigger than rubber tires."

"I have not asked for anything."

"Your eyes ask. You want me to change the *Ordnung* to allow our people to serve in medical situations. And not just any medical situations. In war. On battlefields. Where blood is shed and weapons strike men down. You wish me to say, 'If God Almighty is calling you to serve him as a medic in the army in order to save lives, go and do so. As long as you do not pick up a gun, as long as you reach out to heal friend and foe alike in the Lord's name, go and do so, and may Christ bless.'"

Naomi didn't move a muscle. "*Ja*. That is very well put."

He grunted. "Very well put, eh? So I have been thinking about these things. But it would have to be very well put indeed to convince our ministers and our people. We would lose many families. We might lose all the families."

"Not all."

"Who can say? Certainly it would split our community in two. No matter how carefully I chose my words."

"If everyone could read these letters from mothers and fathers and wives and sisters…"

"Everyone? You would let the whole church read these letters?"

Naomi sat even straighter. "*Ja*."

"The leadership? Even Minister Yoder?"

"There is no shame in those letters. Only honor."

He took off his glasses. "Honor? Is that what you want me to tell Minister Yoder? Doesn't that smack of pride and vanity?"

"They that honor me I will honor."

He stared, taking her words in.

"First Samuel, chapter two, verse thirty," she added.

"I know." Again he looked out the window. Then he got up. "Leave these with me, if you will. I can promise nothing. So rarely the *Ordnung* changes. And in matters that touch on war it never changes."

"This is not about war."

"Not about war?"

"There is making war and there is healing war. They are not the same thing. Would Jesus stand by and watch the man on the road to Jericho bleed to death?"

"Child—"

"Would you? Even if he wore a uniform? Or would you hurry past on your way to church?"

The bishop heaved out his breath as if it weighed hundreds of pounds in his chest. "Enough. I will share the letters among a few. We will see what God does. For he is a good God but also a strange God when it comes to what he will bless and not bless. That is all I can do. Good day, *dochter*."

"Bishop Fischer—"

He opened the door, and a gust of wind brought in the winter cold. "Good day, *dochter*. Go with God."

The drive home was slow and icy. She didn't unharness the mare at the farmhouse because she wasn't sure if Micah would be using the buggy again that day. She gave Maria some oats and went in, stamping the snow off her boots in the doorway.

Rebecca looked up from a pan of bread she had just pulled from the oven. "How is it with you?"

Naomi unwound her scarf and took off her coat. "Oh, who knows?"

"How is our bishop?"

"Well enough. I showed him the letters."

Rebecca bent and put fresh loaves into the cookstove. "I thought you would. How was he with them?"

"He says the *Ordnung* never changes when it comes to matters of war."

"Of course. What did you expect him to say?"

"I expected him to open his eyes. I expected him to open his heart."

"Naomi, honestly."

Naomi flared. "Why not? Is God Old Order Amish? Might he not have something new to say to the people? Might he not want to change a few minds? Soften a few who inside themselves are stone?"

"You're asking a lot of one bishop, no matter how kindhearted he is."

"I'm not asking for the moon. I'm only asking for God to have more of a say in this than the *Ordnung*. I'm asking—"

She stopped abruptly.

Rebecca glanced over as she straightened up, closing the oven door. "What? What is the matter?"

She followed Naomi's gaze.

Luke was standing fully dressed at the bottom of the staircase.

# Eight

"Luke!"

Naomi ran and threw her arms around him, kissing him. "You're up...you're all right!"

Luke's arms remained at his side. When Naomi pulled back to look at him, he didn't smile or speak. But his eyes showed more light than she had seen since the accident. He glanced at Rebecca, who had started toward him and stopped. He looked from her to the fresh loaves of bread cooling on the counter. Then he walked past his sister and Rebecca and sat down at the kitchen table. The two women glanced at each other and at him.

"What is it?" asked Naomi. "What do you want, Luke?"

Rebecca went to the cookstove. "I'm pretty sure he wants coffee and some fresh bread with butter and jam."

She filled a mug with coffee and set it in front of him. He looked at it but didn't touch it. Rebecca cut two thick slices of bread, put them on a plate, and brought it to him along with homemade butter and blackberry jam. Luke made eye contact with Rebecca, and she felt a warmth there. He turned in his chair and fixed his eyes on his sister.

"Cream and sugar. That's what he wants," she said with a quick laugh. "He always has to have his cream and sugar."

She took cream from the icebox while Rebecca gave him the sugar bowl. Once he had both in front of him, he put three heaping spoonfuls of sugar in the coffee and poured in a generous amount of cream, stirring them together until the black coffee was a muddy brown. Then he picked up the blue mug and began to drink.

Though he still seemed to be far off in the distance, Naomi couldn't resist mussing his brown hair and smiling. "My sweet brother and his sweet coffee."

She was rewarded by Luke shifting his eyes from his coffee and its curl of steam to her face. A small movement of his lips lifted both corners of his mouth. A surge of happiness, flashing light as if it were silver, went through Naomi's chest.

"Thank you, Lord," she said out loud. "This is much more than I expected, and it comes much sooner as well." She hurried to the parlor. "Is Micah in here?"

"No," Rebecca told her. "He went out to the barn."

"I must tell him."

Rebecca smiled. "Another emergency?"

Naomi hadn't removed her coat and was quickly out the door. "*Ja*. Don't you think so?"

She found her husband grooming several of the horses inside the large gray barn.

"Micah. Forgive me. I must speak. Luke is up!"

He gave her a puzzled look, stopping what he was doing, brush in hand.

She laughed. "I'm sorry. I mean to say he's up on his own and dressed. He came downstairs from his room without any help and now he's sitting at the table drinking coffee and eating bread and jam. We must tell the doctors. And the bishop and the ministers."

Micah instantly put the brush on a shelf behind him and ran for the house. As he passed his wife he reached out and gave her arm a squeeze. She followed him inside. Even from across the room she could see fresh life come into Luke's dark brown eyes as Micah rushed in and wrapped his arms around him, lifting him from his chair. Slowly Luke's arms went around Micah in return. Naomi had already cried so much that morning, reading the letter of the young soldier's mother, she didn't think she had anything left inside her. But tears slipped down her face just the same.

"All of us should have coffee." Rebecca brought the large pot to the table and put it on a coaster. "And bread. And cheese. It's lunchtime."

Micah sat down next to Luke for a few moments, smiling into his face and gripping his shoulder. But when Rebecca and Naomi brought cheese and roast beef to the table, he immediately got up, shook Luke's hand, and went to the parlor with his plate of bread and meat and a cup of coffee.

Rebecca bowed her head. "Thank you, Lord, for the fruit of the earth and the labor of our hands, which you have blessed. Thank you that Luke is once again sitting at the family table. In Jesus Christ our Lord. Amen."

Luke stared at Naomi as she began to butter a slice of the white bread. She tried to read his expression but didn't understand what he was saying to her until he flicked his eyes to the parlor door and back to her.

"I'm sorry," she said. "I don't know how much you remember. You were in an accident."

His head seemed to move slightly as if in a nod.

"It was very bad. A car struck the buggy. Mama and Papa—" She couldn't finish the sentence and hung her head a moment. Then she tried again. "It was on the way into Lancaster. The car collided with our buggy. The horse was killed. Mother and father were killed. Ruth was killed. You were thrown clear and hit your head. Other than that, you weren't terribly hurt. But your head injury was bad enough. You have been in bed. Hardly able to move. It's because of the injury you're not speaking."

He set down his coffee and left the rest of the food on his plate untouched, focusing all his attention on her.

"Now it is only you and me in this house, you and me and our dear friend Rebecca, who I've asked to live with us for a while. Micah, you may remember, enlisted in the army last year and went to Afghanistan as a medic. Now he is back, I thank God, and is living here as well."

Luke's dark eyes continued to ask the question that had launched Naomi into her lengthy explanation of what had occurred since the crash.

"Luke, Micah was placed under the *bann* because he went to war. You know that's what our people do when someone breaks the *Ordnung*. Even though he has returned, he's not been welcomed back into the community. If he would repent of what he did, the *bann* would be lifted. But he hasn't and he says that he won't. He tells us he believes God called him to go to war to save the lives of the wounded. *Ja*, he said this to the bishop and the entire leadership. So the *bann* remains in force. He can't speak with us, nor can he eat with us. Even though we're husband and wife, we can't share the same room, can't touch. That's why he's in the front parlor and we're sitting here."

Luke's eyes remained on her.

"Oh, Luke." She rubbed her hands over her face. "Micah and I love being part of the Amish community. Both of us want to remain Amish. Our roots are here. Our childhoods. *Ja*, we believe our future is here too despite the difficult circumstances we're living under right now. So we're abiding by the *bann* and praying God will work things out somehow. It looks impossible to me. But seeing you up on your feet and moving around on your own seemed impossible to me a few weeks ago, and look at you now.

So the God who has set you free can set Micah and me free as well, can he not?"

Another question formed in Luke's eyes. It felt strange to Naomi to be conversing with her brother in this fashion, but it also felt strange that she seemed to be able to understand what he conveyed through his face and eyes.

"You haven't heard Micah's arguments. I happen to agree with him. I think Rebecca does as well."

Rebecca nodded, sipping her coffee. "I do, Luke."

"So that's not an issue between him and me," Naomi went on. "However, we haven't been able to convince the leadership. That means Micah will be shunned until he confesses he was wrong. But he asks us how he can in good conscience say he was wrong to save the lives of men and women injured in battle." She shrugged. "What can I say to that?"

After he ate, Luke wandered about the house, looking in every room and examining different objects. Several times Naomi and Rebecca watched tears form in his eyes. He picked up an old face-less doll Ruth had played with as a child, his father's pipe, and his mother's sewing kit and took them upstairs to his room. Naomi followed him and watched as he arranged the doll and pipe on his bookcase and placed the sewing kit on his bedside table. Then he lay down on his bed and closed his eyes.

*Please let the healing continue, Lord,* Naomi prayed. *Inside and out.*

She walked across the road to where a small wooden hut held a telephone and called the doctor's office to explain what had occurred and make an appointment. After that she drove the buggy to the bishop's house to tell him Luke was up and around but still silent. He praised God and prayed with her and said he and the ministers would come over the next afternoon. Returning to the house, she found Luke still napping and began to help

Rebecca make supper. At five o'clock she wiped her hands on a cloth and smiled at her friend.

"Three at the table and one in the parlor. I'll wake Luke and fetch Micah if he doesn't come in from the barn on his own."

Micah was walking in the door and thumping the snow off his boots when Luke trailed his sister down the staircase. Micah smiled at them and served himself a bowl of cabbage soup along with a plateful of scalloped potatoes and corned beef and peas. Rebecca followed after him into the parlor with coffee and a roll.

"Thank you, Father, for food and shelter this night," prayed Naomi at the kitchen table. "Thank you for the family you've given us here. In the name of our Lord Jesus Christ. Amen."

Luke began to eat and then stopped. Naomi saw his eyes travel to the parlor door and back to her.

"He must eat alone," Naomi reminded Luke. "We're not to speak with him. That is the *Ordnung*. Micah has agreed to abide by it."

His eyes locked onto hers and seemed to catch fire. He took his bowl and plate and stood up, crossing to the parlor and going in. Rebecca and Naomi looked at one another. Naomi took Luke's coffee to him. When she entered the parlor, the two men were eating side by side. Micah looked up and smiled at her. Luke kept his head down and spooned the soup into his mouth.

"What are they doing?" Rebecca asked once Naomi had returned to the table.

"Abiding by the *Ordnung*," Naomi replied, cutting her corned beef with a fork and knife. "Both are eating in silence."

# Nine

A day later Luke marched into the house ahead of his sister and headed up the staircase to his room, still wearing his coat and boots. Rebecca looked from him to Naomi, who was unwinding her black scarf.

"What did the doctors say?" asked Rebecca.

Naomi shrugged, her face tight. "They're happy with Luke's progress. To a point. They felt the BZD regimen should have loosened his tongue by now. So they're talking about stronger medication that can have severe side effects. Or shock treatment. I said no to both. And so they tell me I have doomed my brother to a lifetime of silence."

"Did they speak with Luke himself?"

"*Ja*. As well as they could."

"Did he respond at all?"

"*Ja*, sure. When they talked about stronger pills he got up and left the room."

"Ah. So then you're doing what he wants."

"And what I want. But not what the doctors want."

"How bad can the side effects be?"

Naomi's face grew more rigid. "Bad."

"Then you've done the right thing. We have prayer. And love. And faith. Let's see how far those will take us."

"I hope they'll take us a lot further than we are right now."

Naomi spotted Micah in the parlor doorway, winter jacket buttoned to his neck, flecks of hay on the arms and collar, coffee in his hand, listening to her. Their eyes met and remained on one another. A warmth suddenly spread through her entire body from head to foot. He drained his cup and came and put it by the sink. Stepping past her, he opened the door and headed outside. A final look from him caused a flush to sprout from her neck up over her face.

Rebecca smiled. "Even in silence our men can tell us things."

Naomi put a hand to her cheek, embarrassed by the heat she could feel there. "So it would seem."

"There may be a *bann* against you two eating together or speaking together, but no *Ordnung* can ban my brother from being your husband or from loving you. I see by the way he looks at you that he's proud of you—of how you're standing by Luke, of the strength God has given you, and of the grace in your heart. *Ja*, he's proud of you in a good way." She returned to her pan of cinnamon buns, using a butter knife to spread frosting over their tops. "Proud. And in love. More in love than most husbands in our community."

Naomi's face flamed a deeper red and cut at her skin with a stronger heat.

"When did you say the bishop and ministers are dropping by to pray with Luke?" Rebecca asked to change the subject.

"Oh." She continued to stand in the doorway. "It will be after lunch." She crossed the floor and sat at the kitchen table, still wearing her coat. "It's not just to see Luke. They will talk to me about the cards and letters. Perhaps they'll even wish to see Micah, to ask if he's had a change of heart. Of course I could ask the same of them."

"Please don't. I can't have you under a *bann* too. It would be quite impossible if I were the only one who could speak in a house of four people. It would feel like a tomb." She gave Naomi a cinnamon roll that was so warm the frosting had begun to melt down its sides. "Here. Perhaps this will sweeten your tongue so that you'll only smile and nod when the bishop arrives."

Naomi picked away a strip of the roll and nibbled on it. "How many miracles is it you want God to perform for us?"

"Why? Does his well ever run dry of grace?" She put a cinnamon roll on a plate and handed it to her. "Take this to your husband."

"My husband? All right."

Rebecca smiled. "It's not an emergency, so no talking."

"*Ja, ja. Nicht redden.*"

Micah wasn't in the barn. She took the well-beaten path through the snow to the fenced pasture, where she soon spotted him pitching hay to the beef cattle, throwing it over the wooden rails. For a moment she stopped just to enjoy the smooth rhythm of his movements and his easy strength. Then she approached with the plate as if she were holding a whole cake in her hands. He didn't notice her. She set it down in the snow a few feet from him, but he still didn't turn to look.

*So what is it acceptable to do about cinnamon rolls in danger of freezing when your husband is under the* bann?

"Hey!" she shouted at one of the steers that was being pushy. "*Kastrierten Bullen Geist! Wohnin du gehst!*"

Micah snapped his head around. She coughed. He saw the plate with the cinnamon roll on it. She glanced up at the sun, which was making its way through a great white heap of cumulus clouds, turned without making eye contact, and began walking back to the farmhouse.

"Hey!"

She stopped and looked back.

"*Nicht, die gut schmecken?*"

He wasn't talking to her, but to the steers as they ate the hay and he ate the roll.

*Doesn't that taste good?*

She smiled and carried on to the house.

When she closed the door behind her, Rebecca asked, "So did you find him?"

"*Ja.*"

"And you gave him the cinnamon bun?"

"*Ja.*"

"Without speaking to him?"

"I didn't speak to him."

"Truly?"

Naomi hung her coat on a peg. "I spoke to the steers."

Rebecca put her hands on her hips. "*Vas?* What are you talking about?"

Naomi smiled and shrugged. "Let's make some lunch and then prepare for the meeting with the leadership."

⤳∽⤲

Bishop Fischer and the ministers came in from the bright December sunshine and blazing snow with smiles and a spattering of laughter, immediately asking to see Luke. He was waiting for them, seated at the kitchen table, rising to his feet as they removed their coats and hats and entered the house. They took his hand, and he returned their handshakes weakly but, Naomi noticed, with a trace of warmth in his eyes. The bishop and Minister Yoder hugged him, all the while praising God in German, and Luke raised his arms high enough to put them around their lower backs.

"Wonderful. Thank God." The bishop gripped both of Luke's hands. "Let us pray with you."

The ministers gathered in a circle and bowed their heads as Bishop Fischer began. When he was finished, the others prayed, one after the other, Minister Yoder bringing it to a conclusion with one large hand resting on Luke's shoulder. Then they sat at the table and helped themselves to the coffee and cinnamon rolls laid out before them.

"We trust you'll have your voice back soon too, eh?" Bishop Fischer smiled at Luke as he brought his coffee to his lips. "Always you sang well. I could always make you out no matter how many were singing at the same time."

Luke sat and listened to him, not drinking his coffee.

The bishop leaned back and caught Naomi's eye. "The ministers have read your letters."

Naomi nodded.

"I would have brought them back to you, but you said I should let any of our people read them who felt an inclination to do so."

She nodded again.

"So that will take several days as they circulate among the families." He ran his fingers through his beard. "There will be no one who doesn't thank God for the lives saved, no one."

"But that is not the point of the *bann*." Minister Yoder folded his hands and rested them on the table near his half-eaten roll. "It's the breaking of the *Ordnung* that has brought about the problem between your husband and the church. Not saving lives. For how could we censure someone for protecting the sanctity of human life?"

Naomi kept her eyes down, looking at white drops of spilled cream and sprinkles of white sugar scattered over the table's wooden surface. "If he hadn't gone to Afghanistan, he couldn't have saved the men and women whose mothers and wives write to me."

"God would have ordained others to do the work. He would have brought someone who is not Amish. Someone not called to be an Amish witness in the world," rumbled Minister Yoder.

"Except God called him to the war zone."

"He says."

Naomi lifted her eyes. "So you don't think God could give you or anyone here a command that would go beyond the rules of our church?"

"No."

"The man-made rules?"

Minister Yoder shook his head. "No."

"So the Pharisees and religious rulers also thought."

Rebecca looked at her friend in surprise and alarm, eyes widening, and quickly spoke up before Minister Yoder could reply. "My brother gave us his reasons for his conduct."

Minister Yoder was scowling at Naomi, lines deepening around his eyes. He didn't look at Rebecca. "We have heard the reasons."

"Suppose—"

Yoder cut Rebecca off. "Suppose, suppose. *Ja*, that's how your brother talks. Suppose, suppose. We are not in a fairy tale, I thank God."

"But if there was a gang fight outside our doors and men lay wounded in the ditch—"

He snorted. "You and Micah and your drug gangs. They are in Pittsburgh and Philadelphia. Not here. They will never come here."

A hint of steel came into Rebecca's voice. "Jesus told his parables. I will tell mine."

Yoder grunted but said nothing.

"The wounded men are bleeding at the side of the road—"

"Yes, yes," the bishop interrupted. "It is as Minister Yoder says. We have been through all this before. We would call nine-one-one from the phone in the hut. We would try to stop the bleeding. We would do all we could to save them."

"But that's what my brother did."

"Your brother traveled to a combat zone. That's a far different matter. We merely take care of our neighbors."

"Christ taught that all men are our neighbors."

The bishop waved his hand. "It's always apples and oranges. By helping the military wounded, Micah supported the war effort. By helping the wounded in your parable, we support nothing except the right of those made in God's image to live and discover his grace."

"The soldiers can also be healed and live and find his grace."

"It supports the war effort. We cannot support a war directly or indirectly."

Naomi spoke up, hands folded on the table like Minister Yoder's. "If you help the wounded of the drug gang, you help the sale of illegal drugs. How wicked is that?"

"*Vas?*" rumbled Minister Yoder.

"If you help a wounded man who is an atheist, you help unbelief grow. If you help a woman who is in favor of abortions, you help the practice of abortions to continue unabated. If you help a teenager who is a thief, you support robbery. Isn't that what you are saying when you accuse Micah of spreading war by saving soldiers' lives?"

Into the silence came the tapping of Bishop Fischer's fingers.

Naomi spoke again. "We might as well not try to save anyone's life except those who are Amish in good standing and not under any *bann*."

The bishop raised his hand. "*Genug*. Enough." He pushed back his chair. "I cannot say what our people will do about the letters. We shall meet again in a week and let you know. Yet the decision rests on us, the leadership God Almighty has put in place, when it comes to matters of the *Ordnung*. *Ja*, and especially on my head. I will have the final say. So it is with our people. The responsibility is great. May not my soul hang in the balance? What if I should lead hundreds astray? Thousands? It is a weighty thing. You have your clever arguments. I have four hundred years of God's command to our people—the Amish shall not kill." He got to his feet. "Or aid those who kill."

The ministers rose. So did the two women. Luke remained in his seat.

# Ten

The next morning Rebecca called down to Naomi from the head of the staircase. "So where is Luke? He's not in his room or in the parlor."

Naomi glanced up from her sewing. "Oh, he's helping Micah with the cattle." She smiled. "Would you believe it? I even saw him pitching some hay a half hour ago."

Rebecca came down and sat by the front window and picked up her own sewing, a dress of hers that had torn on a nail. "When it comes to Luke, *Gott ist auf der Uberholspur.*" *God is on the fast track.*

"Not so much with Bishop Fischer and Minister Yoder or the others," mumbled Naomi as she worked on a pair of her husband's pants.

"They're harder to deal with than Luke."

"And that's surprising. Doesn't our leadership walk with God?"

Rebecca shook her head as she threaded a needle, one eye shut. "Bite your tongue, or your words will bite others."

"Hm." Naomi held up the pants to look at them better. "I need to take them in a couple of inches."

"Don't bother. We'll fatten Micah up in no time."

"That won't be so easy. When I walked by the barn the other day he was doing push-ups."

"In the barn?"

"And when I came back that way he was using a low beam to do chin-ups."

Rebecca snorted. "The army. Give him time and he'll become as lazy about exercise as the rest of the men."

"I wonder. He can be very stubborn and determined."

"*Ja*, well, we've seen that. He's still under the *bann* because of that."

A shrill whine pierced the glass and entered the house.

"The dirt bike." Naomi put down her sewing. "Timothy Yoder."

"*Rumspringa*."

"But there is snow down."

"Not much. A great deal of it has melted over the last couple of days. Anyway, you can see the gravel road is clear enough." Rebecca lifted her eyebrows. "So if Minister Yoder can indulge his son with a dirt bike, perhaps he's not immoveable after all."

"Oh, he'll say dirt bikes are one thing, but going to war is something else again. Apples and oranges." She imitated his growl. "*Rumspringa* is *rumspringa*, a vow at baptism is a vow at baptism, war is war."

"Hush, Naomi."

"He will. You watch."

"I'm not going to watch your next spat with Minister Yoder because there's not going to be one, *ja*? It won't help you to argue with him. That won't win him to your side."

"He'll never be won to my side. So what does it matter if we have a good discussion?"

"Discussion? Is that what you call it?" Rebecca folded her dress. "Now, what else is in the sewing bag?" She glanced out the window again. "So he has an audience now. That's why he's showing off."

Naomi saw the small crowd of thirteen- and fourteen-year-old boys who were watching Timothy Yoder do spins and leaps with his bike. Behind them stood three older girls.

"Ah. Sarah Harshberger is there. Pretty Sarah with the golden hair and golden eyes. That's why he's practically doing somersaults."

Rebecca stood up. "I'll bring the sewing bag here. Maybe we can both empty it before we start supper." She walked away, still talking. "If we weren't the last farm in the row, we wouldn't have to listen to that racket. It's because there is all this open road and no farmhouses but ours that Timothy is here. Minister Yoder probably sent him this way on purpose."

"Ha." Naomi hunted for a spool of thread in a container at her feet. "To punish us?"

"To rattle our brains until we have some sense. *Rumspringa* is *rumspringa*, a vow at baptism is a vow at baptism, war is war, a dirt bike at Christmas is a dirt bike at Christmas."

"*Ja, ja.*"

Rebecca went upstairs. Naomi watched Timothy spin his bike in tight circles, making sure he sprayed Sarah and her friends with slush. They laughed and squealed and ran away. He called out to them, grinning, and then gunned his engine and raced in the opposite direction, taking a wide ditch with a high leap, twisting once in the air, and landing in a field of mud and ice. The girls came back to watch, and Sarah was clapping her hands. He walked his bike farther out into the field, straddling it with both legs, and then turned and faced them, revving his engine till it shrieked. Mud flying out from under his tires, his whole bike fishtailing, Timothy headed back for the ditch, lifting his bike into the air.

"Oh!"

Naomi saw that his takeoff from the muddy field was not good. The bike struggled and then flipped. Naomi gasped as Timothy hit the ground first and the bike landed on him. She then saw a quick spray of blood. She jumped to her feet. Sarah began to scream.

"What is it?" Rebecca had run to the head of the staircase. "What has happened?"

Naomi was racing for the door. "Timothy has crashed. The bike landed on top of him."

Naomi didn't even put on a coat. She ran from the farmyard and down the lane to the road. Sarah was still screaming. All of the boys had gathered around Timothy and the bike. He wasn't moving or getting up. One of the boys turned away and fell down in the mud and snow, his hand over his mouth.

"*Helfen Sie uns bitte!*" Sarah was crying. "*Helfen Sie uns bitte!*"

Naomi saw men in their black clothing and hats running from their barns and yards and coming down the road as quickly as they could. She would get there well before any of them, but she had no idea what she should do.

*Get the bike off him. First of all, get the bike off him. God help us!*

She heard the sound of boots. Micah pounded past her faster than she had ever seen any man move. In seconds he was far ahead of her, the back of his black coat flapping. She had always been the quicker of the two, but she could not catch him.

*What has happened to you? Who are you now?*

Suddenly as she ran after him, for one long moment, everything around her changed. The melting snow was gone along with the mud and the chill in the air. The sun beat like a hammer on her back, and the glare off the sand and rock forced her to squint. Heat waves rose up from the ground, making Micah shimmer and the children at the accident scene waver and disappear. She couldn't get her breath it was so hot, and the air stung the skin on her face and hands.

*What is this, Lord? Vas ist los?*

Micah was wearing a helmet and his army uniform with the desert camouflage. When had he changed clothes? He wore a pack on his back and carried a smaller one in his hand. His boots were the same color as the sand. In front of them, through the smoke, Naomi saw an armored vehicle lying on its side. Men were underneath it. Someone was yelling and yelling. She kept running.

*I don't understand.*

She saw soldiers coming across the desert toward the dark smoke. They threw themselves to the ground as the sand erupted in front of them. She heard whining and zinging sounds but didn't know what they were. In front of her, rocks and stones sprang into the air around Micah's boots. A tear suddenly opened on his sleeve, and he spun sideways and staggered. But he quickly recovered and kept on running, crouching, smoke still boiling up black from the wreck of the army vehicle he was headed toward. She heard a loud cracking that was sharp and rapid.

*Gunfire!*

Now she understood Micah was running through a storm of bullets and she was right behind him. The armored vehicle had detonated a mine or been hit by a rocket, things Micah had told her about. He was the only soldier who was up on his feet. Others were hugging the desert floor and firing back at an enemy she could not see. A roar filled her head. A helicopter darted in, its machine guns spitting fire, turning the desert beyond the wreck into huge clouds of sand and dust. The wash from its blade and its speed ripped the *kapp* from her head and tore at all her hair, unraveling it, twisting it, tangling it. She fell to her knees, stones biting into her flesh.

*I cannot run anymore.*

But Micah kept on until he reached the wreckage. She watched him bend over one body after another. Blood had soaked through his left sleeve. She saw him take gauze and needles out of his pack. Bullets rang out on the steel on the burning vehicle. He ignored the near misses and continued to work on one of the wounded soldiers.

*You are doing this. You are the one doing this. No one else.*

"Naomi! Quick! I need your help!"

Micah had pulled the bike off Timothy and thrown it to one side. She dropped to her knees by the boy. Micah grabbed her hands and clamped them down over a wound that was pumping blood under the shoulder.

"You must use all your strength, do you understand?" He kept his voice calm. "You must control the bleeding. All right?"

She stared at Timothy's torn and damaged body and didn't respond.

"Omi." His voice was quieter. "Listen to me. I need you to stop the bleeding. I'm going to take my hands away and deal with other things. You must keep up the pressure."

She blinked. "*Ja.*"

"I'm taking my hands away. Are you pressing down?"

"*Ja.*"

"Hard?"

"*Ja, ja.*"

She pushed down as hard as she could. Blood oozed up between her fingers, and she put her shoulders and back into it. Micah put his ear by Timothy's mouth while he ripped a patch off his jacket with a pocketknife. He placed the patch over a wound on the other arm. He glanced around.

"Sarah?"

Sarah was standing nearby, tears covering her face.

"Sarah. I need you to hold this patch in place for me."

"It's my fault. He was doing it for me. He wanted to show me."

"He will get better. If you help me with this wound he will get better."

"I'm no good at this."

"Hold this patch with your hands like you see Naomi doing. Please."

She squatted by Timothy, the tears still coming, and awkwardly put her hands on the black patch and his wound.

"A bit harder, Sarah. That's right. You're doing very well."

Rebecca ran up, her breath coming in gasps. "I called nine-one-one—from our phone hut—"

"Thank you, sister." Micah peeled off his coat and draped it over Timothy. "Can I have your jacket?"

"*Ja*—of course—"

She took it off and gave it to him, and he placed it on top of his coat.

"Do you need another, Mr. Bachman?" asked Sarah.

"Two or three more would be good."

"Someone pull mine off me." She looked up at her friends. "Lydia. Deborah. Go ahead. Just do it fast. Start with my left arm. I'll keep my right hand on the wound."

"You'll freeze," Lydia protested.

"I won't freeze. It's not that cold out."

"You'll get chilled."

"And Timmy will die. Take it off me."

Her friends tugged off her navy blue coat and put it on Timothy. Then they added their own.

Micah was cutting a long strip off his pants that he used as a tourniquet above the knee on the boy's right leg. The men came rushing up as he was cutting another to wrap over a fracture on the other leg.

"What is happening?" one of the men asked.

"What can we do?" asked another.

"I need two more coats on top of the boy to keep him warm."

All five of them unbuttoned their coats and placed them over Timothy.

"Someone must get Minister Yoder and his wife," Micah said.

"So I'll get my buggy and drive to their house right away." One of the men left at a run in his shirtsleeves.

"We can help you lift him and get him in front of a fire." A man bent close with his hands on his knees.

"No." Micah shook his head. "We can't move him. He could have a back or spinal injury. We might end up making things worse. Paralyze him."

"The ambulance will take at least ten minutes."

"He's breathing. All your coats will keep him warm. We have the bleeding checked for the moment."

"How bad is he?"

Micah didn't respond. He was gently probing the back of the boy's head. As he did he smiled at Sarah. "How are you doing?"

"I'm all right," she choked out, holding back sobs.

A man crouched by her. "Let me take over."

She didn't look at him. "I'm fine, Mr. Kurtz."

"You must be tired."

"*Nein*, I'm fine," she repeated.

Micah put his ear to Timothy's mouth and then checked his pulse.

"What about you, Omi?" he asked, his fingers against the side of the boy's neck. "Do you need a break?"

She could feel the strain in her arms, but she shook her head. "I'll be here as long as you are."

"*Ja?*"

"I like to see you work. I like to hear your voice."

He looked down at the wounded boy. "Something isn't right. I'm missing something."

Carefully he put his fingers under Timothy's back. On the right side they came away red. In an instant he had his shirt off and was folding it into a wad. Now he only wore his white undershirt and his torn pants.

"We have a large wound." He slowly put the wadded shirt into the hole his fingers had found. "This will help. Mr. Kurtz—"

"*Ja?*"

"Kneel here on the right side of Timothy. Push down firmly here…not too rough…this will put some pressure on the back wound. Keep it up against the dressing I made with the shirt to staunch the flow of blood. Do you understand?"

Mr. Kurtz nodded and took his place, pressing with both hands where Micah showed him.

"Easy," said Micah. "A little less force. Just enough. Good. Perfect. *Danke*."

Naomi watched everything her husband did with the strong eyes of a falcon.

*So this is what you did over there. And this is what you do now. This is Micah Bachman.*

The sound of horses' hooves on the gravel. A man running. Minister Yoder's black beard and glasses and bald head.

"What? What has happened?"

"The bike flipped over on him, Minister," Naomi replied. "We've called for the ambulance."

"No, no, no. What was he doing? Stunts? I asked him, 'Please, no stunts.'" Tears formed behind his lenses. "We must get him into the buggy and back to the house."

"Minister Yoder." Micah was checking Timothy's pulse again. "Your son landed on his back. We dare not move him."

The minister's eyes blackened. "What are you doing here? What are you doing to my son?"

"Trying to stabilize him. Stop the bleeding. Control shock. Keep his airways clear. Make sure he's warm. Watch his heart rate."

"You shouldn't be touching him."

"We had to bandage him, sir. Apply pressure on the worst wounds. Make a tourniquet."

"My son—get away from my son. We put him in the buggy and get him to his bed."

"Minister Yoder—"

The minister put his big hands on Micah's chest and shoved. "Away from him!"

Micah fell back against the dirt bike.

"Stop, Minister!" snapped Mr. Kurtz. "None of this! Shame!"

"He will not—he must not—"

One of the girls pointed. "Now it comes!"

The emergency vehicle wasn't using its siren. It had barely stopped when men and women in uniforms jumped out.

One of the EMS crewmen stared. "What have we got?"

Micah bent over the boy again. "Dirt bike flipped over on him. He landed on his back."

"We need the board!" the crewman called back over his shoulder.

"Pulse is weak but steady. Multiple fractures and multiple wounds. Compound fracture, tibia, left leg. Broken right arm. Bad wound, lower back, right side. Another under the right shoulder. A third on the left arm."

The crewman had his stethoscope out. "Got it."

Two women and another man, all in EMS uniforms, set a bright red board down beside Timothy.

"Need help getting him on the trauma board?" asked Micah.

A woman nodded. "Let me get his head. You can help the others."

"Sue," the lead crewman said to the woman, "we're going to need a number of feeds going as soon as he's secured in the vehicle."

"I'll get them going as soon as we've got him in."

Micah worked with them as if all five had been together for years. Timothy was swiftly secured on the board and slid into the emergency vehicle. Minister Yoder climbed in with his wife. He would not look at Micah.

"Thanks for getting things under control." The EMT shook Micah's hand. "We'll let you know how he does."

"Okay. I'll be down."

"We'll be taking him to Lancaster. May have to fly him into Philadelphia."

"Right."

The EMS vehicle pulled away in a spray of mud and slush.

"You looked as if you were one of the ambulance team," Naomi said. "As if the group of you had been together for years."

"When I disappear into town for hours at a time, I spend it with them. I've been a volunteer."

"I see."

Micah looked at Naomi. "We should go in to the ER."

"I want to come as well," said Rebecca.

"What about Luke?" asked Naomi.

Micah nodded toward the men. Luke was standing with them.

"He's been here all along," Micah said.

"He saw everything?" Naomi asked.

"*Ja.*" He smiled at the girls and young boys and at the men. "Thank you all for your help and your prayers. Make sure you pick up your coats."

They nodded at him.

Sarah responded with a thin smile. "Thank you, sir. I know you made a difference. Despite what Minister Yoder thinks."

"*Danke*, Sarah." Micah threw his coat over his bloodstained undershirt. "Come on." He looked at Naomi and Rebecca and Luke. "Let's harness up Maria and get into town."

"Oh, Micah, we can't take the horse, we must have a driver."

"All right, let's get a driver."

He glanced at the men from the church. "Who will take care of the Yoder children?"

Mr. Kurtz bent down to pick up his jacket. "Martha will already be there. We are the next farm over. I will join her."

"*Gut.*"

Micah hurried across the road, Luke and the two women trailing him. His pace was rapid.

"This is when I wish the Amish had helicopters," he said.

No one smiled. No one laughed. He glanced at Naomi's face. "What?"

Everything about her in that moment—her skin, her eyes, her hair, her face—was either black or white. "It's nothing. Let's just hurry."

"It's something. We won't be free to talk forever."

She stopped in the middle of the road. "So I know who you are."

Micah stopped too. "What?"

"I understand why you were in Afghanistan. I see it clearly."

"You do? Just because of this?"

She was almost at attention. "Only a few can do what you did in that desert and under those guns. God could have chosen only a few. You were one of them. Amish or not, you were one of them. No one else among us could do it, and only a handful of the *Englisch*. So it had to be you. You had to go there. That is who you are, Sergeant Bachman. That is who God made you to be."

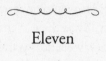

# Eleven

Naomi sat with Rebecca in the waiting room down the hall from ICU. Across from them were Micah and Luke. Sitting in chairs all around were Amish men and women from their church. Some spoke in murmurs and whispers. For Naomi and Micah, the time to talk was over. Except for a few words between the two women, the four sat in silence.

"But we wish to see him again."

"I'm sorry, Minister Yoder. We're preparing him for medevac."

"Once more."

"I'm sorry, sir. He's already out the door and into the chopper."

Everyone looked up as Minister Yoder and his wife appeared in the hallway with the doctor. Bishop Fischer was also with them, but he said nothing. His hand rested on Minister Yoder's shoulder.

"We can see him in Philadelphia, *ja*?"

"Of course."

"And things are well, they are going very well, God be praised?"

"Just as I told you. He is holding his own." The doctor's voice grew so quiet, Naomi could barely hear. "There's no damage to his spinal cord. No paralysis. But there was significant blood loss."

She saw Yoder's face darken. "*Ja*. So at the scene of the accident it was not done right." He didn't lower his voice. "Mistakes were made. People bungled."

The bishop patted his shoulder. "Please, brother."

The doctor looked at Minister Yoder in surprise. "What are you saying?"

"My son would be in better condition but for what was done to him after he crashed, *ja*? He would not even need to be airlifted to Philadelphia, would he? It was there, right at the beginning, that someone who didn't know what he was doing made things worse."

Naomi looked at Micah. He was bent over and had his eyes fixed on the floor.

The doctor looked squarely at Minister Yoder. "I'm not quite sure what you're getting at, but I will tell you this. I don't know who the first responder was when your son had the accident. I don't know who applied first aid before the EMS crew showed up. But whoever it was saved your son's life."

The doctor disappeared back down the hallway.

Minister Yoder's face went from blood red to the color of snow. He watched the doctor as he strode away, looked at his wife and at Bishop Fischer, and then lowered himself into a chair.

Rebecca patted Naomi's knee. "We should go. It will be dark soon."

"Minister Yoder will want people to pray with him."

"It's not us he wants, Naomi."

The four of them got up as other families gathered around the Yoders. Their driver, a young man from an *Englisch* home not far from the farmhouse, got up as well and opened the door. They all walked out into the cool air, where clouds were covering the evening sky.

"Well, not long till Christmas," the young man said as he slid behind the wheel of his van and blew on his fingers.

Micah climbed in beside him. "No, not long."

At home a stew had been sitting in the warming oven. It was a little dry, but Micah and Luke dished up bowlfuls for themselves, cut large pieces of bread from a loaf on the counter, and went into the parlor together to eat together in silence, just as they'd been doing ever since Luke had started feeding himself.

"So what are we to do with Minister Yoder?" asked Rebecca as she ate with Naomi at the kitchen table.

Naomi shrugged with one shoulder. "What can we do? A minister serves for life. We can only pray."

"But even the doctor said Micah had helped—"

"I know."

Rebecca ate for a few moments and then spoke again. "I've wondered about your father, Naomi."

"*Ja?*"

"So he is with the Lord. But he was a minister with us. Shouldn't there be someone to take his place? Someone who might stand up to Minister Yoder?"

Naomi didn't lift her head, scraping the sides of her bowl with her spoon. "They must draw lots. I expect they'll do it at Christmas. But I don't imagine a great deal will change."

"Why not?"

"Because Minister Yoder puts the fear of God in people. I can't think of what another minister could do or say that would calm Minister Yoder down. Likely, he'll become worse because his son is injured. So if he was difficult to take before, he will be impossible now. There's nothing but prayer left for us."

"Well, but that is enough."

"Yes. Amen."

Naomi got up. "Let's clear away the dishes and do the praying. Spend a good hour at it. Read some Scriptures to each other loud enough for Micah and Luke to hear."

Rebecca finished her stew quickly and wiped her mouth with a cloth napkin. "Such a good idea."

A knocking sounded at the door.

"Ah." Rebecca stood up and crossed the room while Naomi loaded dishes in the sink. "It's very late. Who is this?"

She opened the door to Minister Yoder, snowflakes in his beard and on the crown of his wide-brimmed black hat. Behind him a car was running, its headlights making golden tunnels through the swirl of snowfall.

Rebecca stared. "Minister Yoder. *Velkommen. Vas fur eine Uberraschung.*"

He smiled awkwardly, glancing down for a moment. "*Ja*, a surprise, so it is late to be visiting. But my wife and I are on our way to Philadelphia. We will be there a few days…you know, to see our son."

"Of course."

"Still I needed to come by and see your brother. Is he here?"

"My brother?" She opened the door wider. "Please come in, Minister. He's sitting with Luke in the parlor." She half-smiled. "They are both quiet together."

He removed his hat and nodded. "I have permission from the bishop to speak with Micah."

"I see."

He bent to remove his boots.

"No, Minister." Rebecca put a hand on his arm. "Just stamp them. You're in a hurry. That's all right."

"You're sure?"

"*Ja, ja.*"

He hit each boot against the mat twice, and bits of snow fell off. Then he followed Rebecca to the parlor, nodding to Naomi, who was at the kitchen sink but moved to where she could watch everything. In the parlor she could just see Micah sitting with Luke. Both were sipping from their coffees. Surprised at seeing the minister, Micah began to rise, but Minister Yoder waved him down with his hand.

"No, no, stay where you are. This will only take a few minutes. I am allowed to speak with you, you are allowed to listen, all right?"

Micah nodded and sat back down.

"I'm known for being forthright. Over the years I have counted it a blessing. I don't mince words, but speak plainly. And so it is good to speak so. As long as what you say is grounded in truth." He nodded as he looked at Micah. "Of course I had trouble with you enlisting and going to war. We all did. I still have trouble with it. But that is not why I have come."

Naomi had left the sink with its warm water and dishes and saw and heard Minister Yoder from just outside the kitchen. Rebecca stood beside Minister Yoder with a dishtowel in her hand.

"I freely admit I can be stubborn and headstrong," Minister Yoder continued. "Two of my many faults the Lord is working on by day and by night. I am here to apologize for my actions on the road. I yelled. I accused. I pushed you with my hands as hard as I could. My behavior was unbecoming, especially for an Amish minister." His eyes glimmered. "God forgive me. But I ask your forgiveness as well."

Naomi saw the movement in her husband's eyes and on his face.

"Yet there is more I must say," Minister Yoder rumbled. "Our bishop is fond of saying that God's ways are not our ways and that often enough he doesn't do things in the manner in which we should like to see them done. I find the truth of that in what God has done with your life, Micah Bachman. I said *nein*, and I still say *nein* to your military training, *ja*, even your training as a medic.

"But what happens? My son is fooling around on his motorbike. He has an accident. He could die. What can I do? What can any of us in our Amish community do? So but you are there with your military training. You understand immediately what must be done, for you have dealt with wounded men on the battlefield. I and the others say no to your army training and no to medical work in Afghanistan. But if you had not had your training in the army, if you did not have the experience of treating wounded men in Afghanistan, my son would be dead now. I and his mother would not be traveling to Philadelphia to see him in the hospital.

We would be laying his body out on a table in our house and washing it and clothing it for the funeral."

Naomi couldn't remain where she was any longer. She made her way to the doorway of the parlor. Minister Yoder's big hands were trembling on the hat he held in his hands. Both Micah's and Luke's faces gleamed in the light from the woodstove.

"Who can understand these things? We say what you did was against the *Ordnung*. Yet God uses what is against the *Ordnung* to save a life—my son's life. I, who have been against you from the start, I am the one who is blessed by your disobedience to our rules. You are the one under the *bann* who stops on the road and treats the wounds of the boy whose father agreed with the bishop and ordered the *bann*. How is this possible? Who but God Almighty can bring such a thing to pass? And what am I to do about this? What am I to understand? How am I to change?"

He shook his head.

"I must go. I once again ask your forgiveness, Micah Bachman. You are part of God's work in this world in a way that baffles me, for it challenges so much of what I believe. I must ponder this. I must pray. But somehow, and not only on the road, I have been wrong."

Minister Yoder turned to leave and hesitated. He looked back at Micah. Then he thrust out his hand. Micah got up and took it. Minister Yoder nodded, not taking his eyes off Micah. After several moments he walked from the room, put his hat on his head, opened the door, and went out into the snow and the headlight beams and the dark. In less than a minute everyone inside the house heard the car drive away.

# Twelve

That night Naomi fell fast asleep despite all the thoughts whirling through her mind.

Suddenly, in the middle of a dream, she blinked her eyes.

The room was dark. Something had awakened her.

*Click. Click. Click.*

She sat up.

*Whirrrrr.*

Music began to play—tinny and metallic, but she knew the tune well, a German folk melody that was also used for a hymn.

*Chime. Chime. Chime. Chime.*

"It's four o'clock," she said.

She lit a match.

On the top of her bookcase, a large wooden clock had opened its doors, and a man leading a big gray Percheron out of its stable was moving slowly toward her. He wore a broad-brimmed Amish hat and black pants with suspenders that ran up and over his white shirt. He stopped when he was halfway, as if to encourage her to rise, and then he carried on, the turntable moving him and the horse in a circle back inside the stable and the clock. The doors shut.

*So you fixed it. My wedding present from you. Good for Micah*

*Bachman. I wish you could fix our marriage and the shunning of our church as easily as you fixed this clock.*

She could hear Micah and Luke downstairs getting the wood-stove in the parlor going as well as the one in the kitchen. Then the door opened, and she knew they were going out to the barn. Except for the sound of their boots on the floor and the clang of wood being placed in the stoves, they worked in silence.

*Silence. For the year you were gone, there was nothing but silence. And now you're home, and the silence continues.*

She would get up at 4:30. Until then she liked to lie in her bed and pray and bring Bible verses to mind. First she prayed for the silence to end for both Micah and Luke. After that she prayed for Minister Yoder's son Timothy—he had been in Philadelphia for more than a week and had pulled through. He was doing well, but like Luke, he hadn't spoken, only glanced at his family and those who visited and then looked at the wall or out the window.

*Let him walk again, Lord. Let him speak again. Let him take heart.*

Her prayers took her to Minister Yoder. His apology had been astonishing. Yet in the end it had changed little. The *bann* remained in force. Micah had violated the *Ordnung*, and all the good deeds in the world couldn't alter hundreds of years of tradition.

*Yet Minister Yoder is kind to Micah now, and that's something only you could have brought to pass, Lord. I give you thanks. When he returned from the hospital he came straight to our home to tell us how Timothy was getting along and to say again how grateful he was for what Micah had done—who but you could have brought such a grace into our lives? Still I wish you would break the silences.*

It was a Sunday. She rose and dressed and helped Rebecca make a breakfast of eggs and bacon and oatmeal. As usual, the men ate in the parlor and the women in the kitchen. Luke and Micah returned to the cattle, and Naomi and Rebecca cleaned up and got ready for church. It was being held at the home of Bishop Fischer again.

For a long time the service was only the singing of hymns. At one point Naomi closed her eyes and listened to the men's voices. She imagined Luke's and Micah's among them. Opening her eyes she found that Minister Yoder had stood up and was facing them. He waited for the hymn to end, head down.

"I know we will want to sing to our God much more than this." He removed his glasses and held them in his hand. "And we will. But I must speak. Our bishop and our other ministers know I must speak." He looked from face to face. "About Timothy, you know. Praise the Lord, he gets stronger every day. We pray for his voice, yes, how much we wish to hear his voice again, but he eats, he sits up all on his own without any help from the nurses. We are filled with gladness." He paused, glancing out a window at the sun shining on the snow. "While I was there with my wife I saw other patients in other rooms. Every one of them needed prayer. We spoke with no one but prayed for those we laid eyes on as the Lord directed us."

He looked back at the congregation, and Naomi thought he looked directly at her. "Nearby there was a military hospital. We walked right past it every morning and every evening. Sometimes, when there was a milder day, the wounded soldiers would be brought out in wheelchairs, even flat on their backs, just to take some fresh air, just to see the blue sky and the sun." He nodded. "I felt directed to pray for their healing as well, *ja*, for the healing of the soldiers." His jaw began to quiver. "So the Lord spoke to me one evening and he said, *One of your own people saved some of these. One of your own men kept soldiers here alive. Now you are praying for their healing. Do you not see, the two of you work together?*"

Minister Yoder put a hand over his face. "Last night we drew lots to see who would be minister in place of our brother, Minister Miller, who was taken to heaven. We used different Bibles and we let them fall again and again. Four, five times we did this. Three times it opened to the same book, three times. We saw it as a sign of God's will. But how could it be, how could it be? The book was Micah."

Naomi took in her breath sharply.

Hand still over his face, Minister Yoder continued. "The Lord reminded me of what he had told me on the sidewalk in front of the military hospital. That Micah Bachman and I had striven for the healing of the same men and that both of us had done it in his name. I was under conviction, my brothers. I was under strong conviction, my sisters. So I told our bishop and our ministers what the Lord had said to me, and we fell to our knees and cried out." He dropped his hand. "Do you know what passages the other Bibles opened to? Hm? Do you know? The Gospel of John. There were many words there. But one person had underlined a verse in dark pencil—*Größere Liebe hat kein Mensch als diese, dass ein Mensch sein Leben hingibt für seine Freunde. Greater love has no man than this but that a man lay down his life for his friends.*

The men and women in the room gasped.

"The other Bible had a bookmark, *ja*? We didn't notice it, but when the Bible fell open, we saw it then and decided we must ignore where it had opened because someone had already made sure it would part at that page. But in the end we looked. What do you think, brothers and sisters? Is there a God in heaven? Does he speak to us through his Word? Does he not command us to draw lots for our leaders as the apostles did on the day of Pentecost?"

"*Ja, ja*," the people murmured all around Naomi and Rebecca. "It is how he works among us."

Minister Yoder shook his head. "You would not believe me if I told you what was on those pages. What are we to do? What is your leadership to tell you? On one side is the Lord's Prayer and the Lord's woes against the Pharisees and experts in the law. On the other side the Lord feeds the five thousand, and he is glorified on the Mount of Transfiguration, yes, and he speaks of following him regardless of the cost—we put our hand to the plow and do not look back, for if we do we are not fit for the kingdom of heaven."

There was no sound in the room.

"In the middle our Lord șends out the seventy-two and he comes to the home of Mary and Martha and declares to Mary she has chosen the better part and it shall not be taken from her, it shall not. All of that alone is enough, all of that on its own speaks to our hearts. But there is more. What else is on those pages? What else do we see there?"

Naomi couldn't think. She saw in her mind a Bible open to the Gospel of Luke, she saw the chapter numbers 9 and 10 and 11, but she couldn't read the words.

From behind her, a man spoke up. "And, behold, a certain lawyer stood up, and tempted him, saying, Master, what shall I do to inherit eternal life?"

Naomi stared at Rebecca, her mouth opening, and shot to her feet, turning and stumbling as she looked behind her.

It was Luke.

He continued to speak. "He said unto him, What is written in the law? How readest thou? And he answering said, Thou shalt love the Lord thy God with all thy heart, and with all thy soul, and with all thy strength, and with all thy mind; and thy neighbor as thyself. And he said unto him, Thou hast answered right, this do, and thou shalt live.

"But he, willing to justify himself, said unto Jesus, And who is my neighbor?

"And Jesus answering said, A certain man went down from Jerusalem to Jericho, and fell among thieves, which stripped him of his raiment, and wounded him, and departed, leaving him half dead. And by chance there came down a certain priest that way: and when he saw him, he passed by on the other side. And likewise a Levite, when he was at the place, came and looked on him, and passed by on the other side. But a certain Samaritan, as he journeyed, came where he was: and when he saw him, he had compassion on him, and went to him, and bound up his wounds, pouring in oil and wine, and set him on his own beast, and brought him to an inn, and took care of him. And on the morrow when he departed, he took out two pence, and gave them to the host, and said unto him, Take care of him; and whatsoever thou spendest more, when I come again, I will repay thee."

Everyone had turned to face Luke. Only Minister Yoder, Luke, and Naomi were on their feet. Luke met the gaze of the church with his dark eyes.

"Which now of these three, thinkest thou, was neighbor unto him that fell among the thieves? And he said, He that showed mercy on him. Then said Jesus unto him, Go, and do thou likewise."

Minister Yoder nodded, putting his glasses back over his eyes. "*Danke.*"

Luke remained standing.

The bishop climbed to his feet. "Naomi. Go to your brother."

She made her way past the seats and benches and grasped Luke by his hands. "My brother, what is this?"

"I'm sorry, Naomi. It was time to speak."

"You're sorry?" Tears cut across her face. "You're sorry?"

"They know what God is saying to them. Now they must act on it."

"Why did you come? Why did you come to the worship service today?"

"I felt compelled to put a saddle on Rupert and ride him here."

"And Micah didn't stop you?"

"Why should he stop me? We understand each other." He stared at the bishop. "And you understand the Lord."

Bishop Fischer nodded. "*Ja.* A man can only run from God so long. He can only be Jonah for a season." He looked at the people. "Is it not strange that Luke should speak on such a day as this? On the other hand, why shouldn't the Lord open his mouth on such a day as this?" His eyes swept the men and women seated in his house. "Every married man knows he may be called upon to serve as a minister among us. That if it comes, it will be the Lord who calls him, not his people. The Lord has spoken to us clearly that it is to be Micah Bachman."

Minister Yoder nodded.

Voices rose from the congregation. "But he is under the *bann*!"

"He has broken the *Ordnung!*"

"He cannot be considered, Bishop Fischer!"

The bishop held up his hands as more men spoke up. "All this will be prayed through. All this will be discussed. But I must tell you before we go any further on this Lord's Day, I hereby lift the *bann* on Micah Bachman. I, your bishop, declare he has followed the Lord as the Lord led him even though it led him against the rules of our faith as we have understood them for more than three hundred years. I have prayed, I have fasted, and this is what I declare to you. I am not alone in this. The ministers also feel this is of the Lord. That he called out from among us someone who would bring the healing of Christ into the middle of one of our world's worst hells—warfare. We will not fight God on this any further. We will not resist the Holy Spirit.

"We have our *Ordnung*, and it serves us well. But God has his *Ordnung* too, and it is greater than ours. We bow to it. We all must bow to it. *Ja*, this is what I declare unto you—Micah Bachman may walk among us again and break bread with us again and worship with us again. He may return to his wife and his wife to him. He may speak, and we may hear his voice lifted again in praise to God. Your leadership is in unity on this—Micah Bachman is free."

Murmuring ran through the congregation.

"Naomi, there must be talk among the people over this. Talk that would be best if you were not here. You and Luke return to your home." The bishop turned to Rebecca. "*Dochter*, it is your brother, Micah. It should be me who goes to him and tells him the *bann* is lifted, but this day I ask you to go in my place. I must remain here. Tell him we believe the Lord's will is done and we embrace him again not only as your brother but ours." Murmuring continued in the room, but the bishop ignored it and smiled. "Go in peace, Naomi and Rebecca and Luke. Go to Micah Bachman and rejoice."

Naomi found herself outside the bishop's house with a strong mix of emotions whirling around in her chest and head—happiness at what they would be able to tell Micah, joy that Luke was talking, but sadness and a feeling of gloom at what was going on inside the Fischer home as she stood with Luke and Rebecca in the snow. Happiness and joy won out for the time being, and she threw her arms around Luke and hugged him and laughed.

"Oh, praise God, praise God!" she cried. "I love hearing your voice! God bless you!"

He hugged her back, and his arms around her were tight. "For days I felt as if my tongue would move on its own, but words never came."

"But why today? Why here?"

"I don't know. The bishop can say it is from God. I only know I felt that they would be talking about Micah and that I needed to be there. I had no idea the words would come like they did."

She smiled and kissed his cheek. "Bible words."

He smiled back, a smile that sent even more happiness through her. "Yes. Bible words."

"And now you are speaking as freely as if you'd never stopped."

"I feel okay. I've worked through a lot in my silence." His smile vanished. "I remember pretty much everything."

"I'm sorry, Luke."

"Like I said, I've worked a lot of it through." He glanced back at the house. "What's going on in there?"

"They will argue and debate. They will pray."

"I thought the bishop had the final say."

"He does."

"So?"

"So Amish churches split too, my brother. The leadership will do everything they can to prevent that. But if some families feel the bishop and ministers have erred, they will leave and start their own church. They may even move away to another county." She sighed, her face losing some of its brightness. "No one wants that. Micah will certainly not want that happening on account of him. But it could. Amish communities have been destroyed by such controversies. It's as the bishop told me once—to change the *Ordnung* to permit rubber tires on buggy wheels is one thing, but to change it to lift the *bann* from one who has served in the armed forces, even as medical personnel, without repentance, is something else again. A good number of families won't accept this."

"But it's only Micah Bachman. Only one exceptional case. This changes nothing about the way we feel about war."

"*Ja*, but if they bend the rules for one, they have bent them for all. The *Ordnung* has changed. Some families will stay, but some will surely go."

Luke untethered Rupert. "We will pray. We will go home and pray." A small smile made its way over his lips. "Hop on behind me, sister. Let's get you to Micah. I want to see his face when you run to him and tell him he can hold you in his arms again. In the silence we shared together I saw how much he missed you."

Rebecca drove the buggy toward the road. "Come on, you two. We have news to share."

Naomi climbed up on the gelding and slipped her arms around Luke's chest. "How could you know what he missed or didn't miss? Neither of you spoke to each other."

"After a few weeks of quiet, you begin to realize how unimportant most of our talk is. So few words are needed. The eyes say a great deal."

"So you saw his eyes?"

"I saw his eyes on you."

Naomi smiled and leaned her head against her brother's back, squeezing him with her arms as tightly as she could. "So did I."

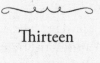

# Thirteen

Naomi jumped down from the horse and ran into the barn. "Micah!"

He spun around, a coil of rope in his hand.

"Micah!" She threw her arms around him. "We can talk! We can hug! The *bann* is ended!"

"What are you talking about?"

"The bishop has announced that the *bann* on you has been lifted."

"What does this mean?"

"It means they believe God called you out from among us to heal the wounded on the battlefield. It means they accept what you have done."

Micah put a hand on her face. "I can't believe it."

"It's true."

"But the others, the church, what do they think?"

"I don't know. But you have the bishop and the ministers on your side, and that's the important thing."

"No—not Minister Yoder!"

"Of course Minister Yoder. You should have heard him speak."

Micah's face split open into a grin. "Is this some sort of miracle?"

"That's exactly what it is."

He put his other hand on the other side of her face. "Look at you. Look at how beautiful you are."

"It's because I'm so happy."

"Well, you always look beautiful. But now it's something special."

"*Ja?*"

Rebecca stepped down from the buggy. "Take this you two and go somewhere far away from here."

"No," protested Naomi. "We shouldn't."

Luke, still in the saddle, said, "Becca's right. Take the buggy and disappear. The next thing you know Minister Yoder will have changed his mind and come running with the *Ordnung* under his arm."

Micah laughed and picked Naomi off the ground. "If he does, just tell him we went to the Amish in Montana. That way he won't find us at the Kissing Bridge."

Blood rushed into Naomi's face. "What are you talking about?"

"You know what I'm talking about."

"Why, even when we were courting we didn't go there."

"So now we're married."

"Even when we were married we didn't go there."

He carried her to the buggy. "So now I'm back from the army and we're out from under the *bann*, and it's past time for us to go there."

"Don't be ridiculous!" Naomi kicked her legs, and snow flew off her boots. "Only the teenagers go there!"

"Well, I feel like a teenager."

"Put me down and we can have a sensible walk in the woods."

"Who wants a sensible walk?" He dropped her in the buggy and climbed in. "Do you want us back for supper, sister?"

Rebecca smiled. "*Ja*, but a very late supper. When more than a thousand stars are out you must come back."

Micah lifted the reins. "*Gut.* I can't count that high, so we will be gone a very long time."

Naomi made a face. "We can't stay at the bridge all day."

"Why not? We have a lot of time to make up for."

"Micah, for goodness sake, we don't need to go to a covered bridge."

"Ah, but here comes Minister Yoder," Micah teased. "Quick. We do need a covered bridge."

Naomi swung her head. "Oh, he is not!"

The buggy pulled out of the yard. "Well, then perhaps we'll meet him at the bridge."

The corners of Naomi's eyes crinkled. "If you'd heard all the nice things he had to say about you, you wouldn't be teasing him like this."

"You must tell me all about it. Every word."

She leaned her head on his shoulder. "Not now. That can wait. Tomorrow will be soon enough."

"You won't forget?"

"You said it yourself—it was miraculous. Who forgets to talk to others about the miraculous?" She kissed him on the cheek. "So but now we're concentrating on something else that's miraculous—you and me permitted to be alone together."

They reached the old covered bridge after a ten minute drive. It had been given a fresh coat of red paint for Christmas. The river it spanned was frozen in parts and still moving in others. Naomi was relieved to see no one else was inside. Like everyone else in the community, she had taken a buggy through it many times and once or twice spotted a carriage or wagon parked in the shadows. This would be the first time she would be one of the ones in a parked buggy.

"Here we are." Micah's face was dark once they were out of the afternoon sunlight. "Is there anything you want to tell me?"

"Besides I love you, you mean?"

"Haven't you missed me as well as loved me?"

"How could I miss you? You've been in the house all along."

"No embracing. No kissing. No soft voices."

"Well, of course I've missed all that."

"Anything else?"

She winked. "The scent of your shaving cream." Her fingers found their way to the beginnings of his beard. "Only on your upper lip of course."

"I think the *Ordnung* should be changed to allow married men to be clean shaven if they want to."

"Oh no, you don't." She slapped him on the arm. "One *Ordnung* change per lifetime is more than enough."

He kissed her softly on both cheeks and both eyes. Then he stopped and held her tightly.

"Is that it?" she asked.

"What were you expecting?"

"Well—a bit more of a windstorm than a breeze."

"I don't feel like a windstorm. It's just sinking in that I can hold you in my arms. I feel so grateful. All I want is to take in the scent of your hair and your skin and feel the warmth of your face."

"I'm only teasing you. I like your gentleness."

His lips brushed her hair, tightly bound up under her prayer *kapp*. "You're perfect, Naomi."

"Oh, Micah, don't get carried away. I'm far from perfect."

"I know you handed those cards and letters to the leadership. I know they made a difference to the *bann* being lifted."

"Not as much of a difference as you saving Timothy Yoder's life."

"All I did was stabilize him. And you helped."

"That's all? That's all you did?" Naomi pulled away and ran her small hands over both sides of his face. "You did it in Afghanistan. Hundreds of times. Now you've done it in Pennsylvania too. Our leadership may be as stubborn as you, but they also have eyes in their heads and wisdom in their hearts. It didn't take them long to make the connection between what you did here and what you did over there. And to realize if they thank God for what you did for Tim, they must also thank God for what you did for the soldiers and their families. It's the same thing."

"But you went to the bishop with those letters—"

She kissed his lips. "It wasn't the letters that changed the bishop's mind or Minister Yoder's mind. It was seeing wounded soldiers with the same eyes they saw Timothy with. Shall God be involved in the healing of Timothy Yoder but not in the healing of the soldiers? Is he only the God of the Amish, or is he the God of all the people of the earth?"

"You sound like a theologian."

She kissed him again, longer and with a bit more force. "It's not for the Amish to be theologians, especially not Amish women. I only know I see the love of God at work in your life. And now the bishop and the ministers see it too."

"What about the rest of the church?"

"That is the Lord's next great task. I'm sure he's up to it." She kissed him a third time. "Just as I'm up to being your wife and companion again."

He laughed. "This doesn't sound very romantic, but I keep thinking I can sit up in bed with you and we can read the Bible out loud together. That I can watch you put your lovely long hair up. That we can sit down and play crokinole and maybe checkers too."

She ran her fingers through his hair. "Oh, all that sounds very romantic to me."

A fourth time her lips found his. "How lonely our lives have been. How painful. But now the world is brand-new. And our old love is a brand-new love too."

Her arms were around his neck and after the fifth kiss she whispered, "I want to go to the house."

"So soon?"

"Not my parents' house. *Our* house. The one we lived in the first year of our marriage. Before you left to join the army."

"Are you serious? But it's boarded up and cold."

"If we stop kissing a moment and you look in my eyes you will know how serious I am."

Micah looked and smiled. "Your wish is my command."

He flicked the reins and steered the buggy out from the roof and walls of the covered bridge and back the way they had come. The December sun had set, and the first stars shone like gems against a sky of dark blue and gleaming bronze. The horse moved at a quick trot.

"How many stars can you count?" he asked.

"There are not a thousand yet."

"So we have plenty of time."

"Oh yes, plenty."

―――

Lanterns and candles were lit in the houses all around, making theirs look cold and black and empty. Micah drove around to the back and sprang down from the buggy. With his hands he gripped the board nailed over the door and pried it loose. Naomi came and stood beside him as he flung the plywood to one side. Then he opened the door with one hand, scooped her up with the other as she laughed and slipped her arms around his neck, and brought her into the farmhouse they had once lived in.

She shivered, still smiling. "Ohhhh, it's colder than I thought."

"Do you want to go to your parents' house?"

"No, I want to stay here."

He placed her down so that her boots settled firmly against the hardwood floor.

"One minute. I'll light a fire."

She grabbed onto his hand. "No, you don't. I don't want a fire."

"But you'll freeze."

"I won't. Hold me. Kiss me. Hug me and hug me in this house where we were newlyweds. That's all the fire I need right now."

"I can't make you as warm as a wood fire, Omi."

Her fingers were playing over his face in the dark. "Yes you can, my husband. I will never be warmer than when I am in your arms. You are like a desert sun. My big desert sun from God."

# Fourteen

The simplest things now gave Naomi the greatest joy.

That evening she sat down at the table with her husband Micah, her brother Luke, and her friend Rebecca, and she felt like a princess in a story with a happy ending. Platters of food were passed, everyone had something to say, and Micah and Luke tucked into the meal as if they were starving. After the plates were cleared the four of them laughed and hooted their way through several games of crokinole, Naomi getting the highest scores while Micah was happy enough just to clear the board of everybody else's counters. After crokinole they all went to a hymn sing at the bishop's house, Naomi's arm linked through Micah's as they sat on a bench in the front room, the first time she had been to a worship service with her husband in more than a year and a half.

"It's perfect, thank God, life is perfect again," said Naomi as they drove back under the stars.

"Now you sound like me." Micah looked up at the night sky. "There are well over a thousand stars out, Becca."

Rebecca spoke from the front, where she sat with Luke, who held the reins in his hands. "It would have been nice if there were a thousand people at the singing this evening. Half the benches were empty."

Naomi closed her eyes. "I'm so grateful for my own blessings, I forget there are other struggles going on. Forgive me."

"I didn't mention this to rebuke you in any way, Naomi. Why shouldn't you thank God and enjoy his gifts to you? Your brother is now well, your husband is at your side, the two of you are finally at church together, soon you will be living in your own house again… no, it would be wrong not to praise the Lord for what you've received. I only say this to remind us that we should pray. I don't know how the rest of our community feels about the change in the *Ordnung*."

"Obviously not too well," responded Luke.

She put a hand on his arm and then withdrew it. "The bishop is coming for coffee tomorrow morning after chores. He can give us a better idea of what's going on. His wife told me he and the ministers spent all afternoon going from house to house."

Micah's mouth formed into a rigid line. "Because of me."

Naomi squeezed his hand. "Because of what God did through you."

—⟡—

Micah and Luke had just come in from looking after the cattle Monday morning when Bishop Fischer drove into the farmyard in his buggy. They entered the house together and sat down at the kitchen table after removing their coats and boots. Rebecca began to pour fresh coffee, starting with Luke and then moving on to the bishop and her brother.

"*Velkommen.*" Naomi set out a plate of chocolate chip oatmeal cookies. "Have you had a busy morning?"

The bishop took four of the cookies, each of which was three inches across, and leaned back with his coffee. "*Ja, ja.* I went to some families and the ministers went to others. We wish to visit everyone before the Christmas service."

"That's a lot of visiting."

He shrugged and raised his eyebrows. "The good work the Lord has given us. The talk is necessary."

Micah folded his arms on the tabletop. "I'm sorry for it."

"What? Sorry for the leadership seeking God's will and finding it? It is we who spoke. You demanded nothing. In our hearts and minds it was settled, and we shared that with the people as we are called to do. Now we ask them to go with us to the place the Lord has appointed."

"And will they?" asked Micah.

The bishop finished a cookie, drank some coffee, and swallowed. "Perhaps not all. Every time the *Ordnung* is affected, people move on to another Amish church or start their own."

"How many will leave?"

The bishop shook his head once. "I don't know. We are praying all the time. There is anger in some, but who knows? The prayers may soften their hearts." He reached to the center of the table and took another cookie. "You must understand, Micah Bachman, that we lost families years ago when I felt the Lord would have us put rubber tires on our buggy wheels—such a blessing for our elderly when it came to the rough spots in the road. But others didn't care about the rough spots. Why could the rough spots not be endured for the sake of following the Amish way as closely as possible? So four families left us and began another Amish church a mile from here. What can we do? The other families stayed and thanked God for the decision."

"How many will thank God for the decision that has favored me?" asked Micah.

"I don't know. But this is not about you. This is about God and whether he reveals his will to his servants, regardless of what that will is, regardless if his will is hard or easy to take. Some say we have been led astray. Others say it is a mistake that must be corrected before Christmas or they will not attend the Christmas Eve service. By that they mean they will stop attending the church altogether."

"And no one has told you what they're going to do for sure?"

Bishop Fischer nodded as Rebecca poured him more coffee. "There are those who say they won't stay unless the decision is reversed and repented of. Others aren't sure but are leaning toward separating from us. What you must not do, young man, is take it upon your shoulders. It is upon God's shoulders. Each member of the leadership is convinced of his word to us—can we go back on that even if all the people leave? Never. Either God speaks or he does not speak, either he leads or he does not lead. This is as basic to our faith as the *Ordnung*—ah, no, it is even more basic, like the earth the fence post is grounded in. We say that God speaks and makes himself clear and that he is not a muddled or wooly-headed God."

The bishop took the cookie in his hand and rapped it on the tabletop. "The Lord reveals his will to his people. Never have I seen our ministers so united in their belief that the *Ordnung* must make room for healers like you, Micah Bachman. And there is no human reason they should be united. Even with his gratitude to you for saving his son's life, Minister Yoder was by no means convinced the *Ordnung* should be altered or, as we say, corrected. No. He was dead set against it. But his testimony on Sunday made it clear how God has changed his heart and his mind and how he used a military hospital to do it. No, this affair is not a matter of human will."

He put the cookie down without biting into it. "You must not take this upon yourself, Micah. That is a sin. God is the one at work, not you, my son. Who knows what he has in store? Perhaps he wishes to begin another Amish church a mile or two away or even next door to me. It may be he is pruning our own church to make it stronger. Suppose this is a test of our commitment to him? There are many possibilities. We can only move ahead in faith and trust our church and our future to God."

He laid his hands palm down on the table. "We must pray. The

Christmas Eve service will be held here in this home. We are not going to hide you away, Micah Bachman, or you, Naomi Bachman. It will be here and the people will come or the people will not come. The church will carry on as it is or it will carry on as a different church. May the Lord be praised in all things, in hard times as well as good times, in winter as well as in spring."

The bishop stood and prayed and sat down. Then Micah stood and prayed. Then Luke. When Luke was done, the bishop got up to leave.

"Micah." The bishop patted him on the shoulder. "We have not touched on the fact you are one of the ministers now. We agreed we would not ask you to visit the families with us. But Christmas Eve shall be your beginning. We will meet for prayer before the service, the ministers and myself, and we ask you to join us."

"Of course. I haven't said anything about it. I was waiting for today, when I knew you would visit, but it's both a surprise and an honor to be a minister in the church. Thank you for including me."

"Ah, it was not an invitation. We had nothing to do with it. No man chose you. It was not about your qualifications or your personality. The lot fell to you just as it fell to Matthias after our Lord's resurrection. Thank God, Micah, not us. It is the Lord's doing, and it is marvelous in our eyes."

Bishop Fischer put on his coat and hat and left. The buggy headed out to the main road, and the noon sun made the snow flash as it sprayed up from the horse's hooves. The four inside watched him go and then looked at each other.

"Now what?" asked Luke.

"Now we pray and read the Scriptures and seek God," replied Rebecca. "And clean the house top to bottom to get ready for Christmas Eve." She grinned at Luke. "Will you help me?"

"Of course I'll help you."

"So first I need a good amount of fresh wood cut and stacked by the woodstove in the parlor."

Luke threw on his coat and was out the door. "I'll have that for you in less than an hour."

She followed him to the door and called after him. "Then I'll need your help to move some furniture!"

"Of course!" Luke called back.

"I can help you with that, Becca," Micah said.

She began to sweep the kitchen floor. "No need. Luke has it in hand. I'm sure Naomi can find something for you to do."

"Oh, I can." Naomi took Micah's hand. "Come with me for a minute."

She drew him into the parlor and shut the door.

"What's all this about?" he asked.

"You can see something is up between my brother and your sister. Leave them alone to work it out. Meanwhile I want to ask you not to fret."

"Who's fretting?"

"You are. About being at the center of the controversy. About causing a windstorm in Amish country. About being asked to serve as minister for life with a church that may split in two before the year is out. Bishop Fischer is right. It's not on your shoulders. It's on God's shoulders and his shoulders are very broad."

"Aren't you concerned about what could happen between now and Christmas?"

The smile left Naomi's face. "*Ja*. I know terrible things could take place. People could fight with one another, people who have been friends for decades. So you and I will pray about that together. We can start right now. But you can't think it's your fault. You can't think you're responsible for what happens to our Amish community here."

Micah put his hands in his pockets, his face dark and cut with the sharp lines of his frown. "It's not a light thing, Naomi. The community could not only split over all this. It could come to an end."

"I know that." She leaned her head against his chest, and he pulled his hands from his pockets and held her. "Believe me, Micah Bachman, I know that very well. We pray, *ja*, we pray. But what will happen? I can't guess."

# Fifteen

It was Christmas Eve.

Naomi lit a final candle while Rebecca put a kettle on to boil water for tea. Luke was arranging benches and chairs in the kitchen and parlor.

Arms went around Naomi's waist from behind, and lips kissed her neck.

"Merry Christmas, my beauty," murmured Micah.

She smiled and leaned back against him. "We may be able to speak and touch now, but we're not alone in the house."

"My sister is playing with the teakettle. And your brother is arranging furniture."

"For people who may never come."

Micah released her. "We've prayed about all that. There's nothing more we can do but hope for the best."

"What did Bishop Fischer say to you this afternoon? I saw him talking to you by the barn."

"He said the leadership would be coming early to pray. Minister Yoder will be bringing his son in a wheelchair."

"*Ja*? He is home now?"

Micah nodded. "It will be good to see him. I haven't laid eyes on Timothy since the accident."

Naomi folded her arms over her chest. "That will be very nice. But what else did the bishop say?"

Micah hesitated. "They've been talking with people all week. The church could lose as many as twelve or fifteen families."

"Twelve or fifteen? But that's half the church—more than half!"

"I know. He said that I'll be included in the leadership and officially a minister from this night on. So I will do my best to help."

"Oh, my. Such news to receive on the night we celebrate our Savior's birth. What else did he tell you?"

"Not much."

"What?"

"Only that…it's time to start growing my beard back since I'm a married man and now a minister."

"Oh." Naomi couldn't stop herself from making a face. "I wish you wouldn't. I like your face the way it is."

"So should we ask them to change the *Ordnung* on this too?"

"Oh, no. I already told you one *Ordnung* change was enough." She took his hand and squeezed it. "I'll put up with it. All good Amish women do."

"Hey, you two," announced Rebecca as she headed to the door. "No more lovebirding."

Naomi let go of Micah's hand. "Who's lovebirding?"

"Why do you think I've been hiding in the kitchen and Luke is still moving benches and chairs around?" She opened the door to Minister Yoder and his son Timothy in his wheelchair. "Tim! It's so good to see you! Welcome! Merry Christmas!" She leaned down and hugged him. "God bless you!"

An awkward smile came and went on Timothy's face. "*Ein gesegnetes Weihnachtsfest.*"

Rebecca laughed in delight. "What? Talking again are we? A blessed Christmas to you too, young man." She hugged him a second time.

Minister Yoder's smile was bigger than Rebecca had ever seen it. "*Ja*, every day he says more and more. We cannot thank God enough. As soon as we brought him home and he saw his dog, that was it, boom, all the words began to tumble out."

"It's wonderful, just wonderful—and at Christmas too."

"*Ja, ja.* It's the only gift we need." He wheeled his son into the house. "You knew we were coming a bit early, *ja*?"

"The bishop told us, *ja.* Why not put yourselves by the fire in the parlor?"

"*Velkommen*," greeted Luke.

"*Velkommen*," greeted Naomi and Micah at almost the same time.

Timothy looked hard and long at Micah's face. He whispered, "I saw you when I thought I was dead."

Lamplight and candlelight flickered over the faces of everyone in the house.

"Your father would have told you I worked on you after the accident," Micah responded.

"*Ja.* But now I see you, and you're the person who is bandaging my leg and telling others where to press down to stop my bleeding, you're the one looking for the big wound in my back. I watched everything you did. I thought I dreamed it. Somehow God let me see with my own eyes everything. Or was it a dream?"

Micah knelt by the wheelchair. "I don't know what it was, Tim. But one thing you need to realize—God was watching over you, God was taking care of you. That's why we're blessed to have you with us tonight."

Timothy stared at him. Then he put out his hand. "Thank you for letting God work through you. Thank you for saving me."

Micah smiled and shook the boy's hand. "It was an honor."

Naomi and Rebecca could see the tears gathering in Minister Yoder's eyes.

"So it is when God has his way with us," he said. "So it is when we turn the things that are impossible and the things we cannot understand over to him." He blinked and looked at the two women. "It doesn't matter what else happens tonight, whether there are ten of us or two hundred. I am blessed."

He wheeled Timothy close to the fire in the parlor.

Over the next fifteen minutes the other ministers and the bishop arrived with their families. Mrs. Yoder showed up with Timothy's brothers and sisters. They remained quietly in the kitchen while the leadership prayed in the parlor with the door shut. They let Timothy remain by the stove. It was the first time Micah was asked to pray with the leaders as a minister. Before he closed the door behind him, he caught Naomi's eye and winked.

*Oh, such a serious time, and you wink.*

But she lowered her head and covered her smile with her hand.

"What will happen?" Rebecca asked the wives of the ministers and the wife of the bishop. "Will the people come here for worship on Christmas Eve? Or is there too much anger? Will they stay away?"

Mrs. Fischer shook her head. "We can't tell. My husband spoke with so many. Who can say if he truly set their hearts at rest? Some may have left us already. Some may stay away to make their disappointment clear."

"Perhaps a dozen will come," said one of the minister's wives. "Perhaps more."

"Or none," said another. "It may be the end of the church."

"So it is not only the men who can pray." Mrs. Fischer bowed her head as she sat in the rocker Micah had repaired. "Heavenly Father, we come before you now and ask your blessing upon our church and our people, for truly it is your church and your people we bring before you."

The women prayed until the parlor door opened. The bishop gestured to them.

*"Kommen Sie bitte hier. Kommen."*

The group of them gathered in the parlor and sat and waited. No one spoke. Naomi took Micah's hand as ten minutes became thirty minutes and thirty minutes an hour. Luke got up and opened the glass door of the stove and fed in more logs. Then he took his seat again. Bishop Fischer took out his pocket watch.

"I'm sorry," Micah suddenly spoke up. "This shouldn't have happened. It would have been better if I had left when I returned from Afghanistan. Then everything would be fine tonight."

The bishop held up a hand. "It would not be fine, Minister Bachman."

Minister Yoder put an arm around his son in the wheelchair. "Timothy would not be with us."

Another minister nodded. "We called upon the Lord. We drew lots, searched the Scriptures, sought understanding. The decision we have rendered regarding you and the *Ordnung* is not only just, it is holy. Never in my whole life have I been so aware that I was being led by God. The others feel the same way. This is what God has brought to pass. Let us see what he will do with it. If we must begin again with the few of us, blessed be his name. It is the Lord's doing and it is marvelous in our eyes."

"Amen, amen," the men and women murmured as the children sat still. "Amen, amen. Blessed be the name of the Lord."

The silence returned, and they sat within it for another half hour, the fire snapping, the candle flames moving back and forth, the faces in the room sometimes black, sometimes gold. Naomi continued to hold on to Micah's hand as the realization that no one was coming and the church was no more sank upon her like a heavy rock.

*It is my fault. I should have done something. I should have gone to the homes. I should have spoken with the women. Talked about the letters.*

Bishop Fischer stood up. "The Lord's will be done. Let us sing carols together. Let us read in the Bible of Christ's birth. All endings in the Lord are beginnings in the Lord. We shall celebrate the birth of Jesus together. The apostles were only twelve in number, but the Lord God made them like a thousand."

Timothy suddenly turned in his wheelchair. "But I hear something."

His father listened too. "No, my boy, there is nothing."

"I hear something."

Naomi frowned. "*Ja*, there is something, but what?"

Luke got to his feet and advanced toward the door.

The rest followed him, and as soon as Luke opened the door, the sound became clear and strong.

"People are singing." Mrs. Fischer narrowed her eyes. "People are caroling."

Minister Yoder wheeled Timothy to the door.

"I can see lights," the boy said.

They saw small bits of flame floating along the lane to the house.

"It is…" Bishop Fischer lost his voice for a moment. "It is our people."

> *Herbei, o ihr Gläubigen,*
> *Fröhlich triumphiernd,*
> *O kommet, o kommet nach Bethlehem!*
> *Sehet das Kindlein,*
> *Uns zum Heil geboren!*
>
> *O lasset uns anbeten,*
> *O lasset uns anbeten,*
> *O lasset uns anbeten,*
> *Den König!*

"So it is 'O Come All Ye Faithful,'" said Rebecca in a hushed voice.

"*Ja*." The bishop nodded. "*Ja*."

*Kommt, singet dem Herren,*
*O ihr Engelchöre,*
*Frohlocket, frohlocket, ihr Seligen!*
*Ehre sei Gott im Himmel*
*Und auf Erden.*

*O lasset uns anbeten,*
*O lasset uns anbeten,*
*O lasset uns anbeten,*
*Den König!*

"What is this?" Naomi asked Micah in a quiet voice. "What does it mean?"

He smiled at her. "I guess it means God isn't quite finished with his miracles yet."

Dozens of people gathered in front of the door and continued to sing the carol—men, women, and children. When they had finished, Mr. Kurtz stepped forward and removed his hat.

"We're sorry we're so late," he said. "We agreed to meet where the lane joins the road and park our buggies there. So but then there were the candles to light and prayers to pray. I'm afraid you thought we might not be coming."

The bishop nodded. "We were not sure. We gave it to the Lord."

"There was much for all of us to work through. Scriptures to read. Prayers to pray. Questions to ask the Almighty." Mr. Kurtz looked at Naomi and Micah. "All the letters have circulated through the people. All the cards. We are not blind. Stubborn, sure, and slow sometimes to see the hand of God when he does something among us he has never done before. But when we see, we see. And when we hear, we hear.

"You would have to be without a heart not to take in the cries of the mothers and wives and sisters who wrote about the lives you saved and the souls you blessed. Does the devil do such things? Does evil bring such kindness to the human race? Can darkness create light? The *Ordnung* is the *Ordnung*, and it is good. But God is God, and he is greater than the *Ordnung* and greater than good. So if he changes our *Ordnung*, we kneel before him and say, 'Your will be done on earth as it is in heaven.' For when we look at what the Lord has done in your life, Micah Bachman, we say two things—we say you are one of us, and we say God is love." He smiled. "So on this night we also say, Merry Christmas, glory to God in the highest."

Naomi was amazed by Mr. Kurtz's words and even more amazed to see all the people nodding their heads and saying amen and breaking into smiles, the candle flames shining on their faces and in their eyes. Micah's arm went around her shoulders, and she leaned against him.

*How is it possible, Lord? How have you done this? How have you taken the heart of stone away and given us all hearts of flesh and blood and spirit?*

The people began to sing again. And as they sang they began to come into the house.

> *Stille Nacht, heilige Nacht,*
> *Alles schläft; einsam wacht*
> *Nur das traute hochheilige Paar.*
> *Holder Knabe im lockigen Haar,*
> *Schlaf in himmlischer Ruh!*
> *Schlaf in himmlischer Ruh!*

And she sang "Silent Night" with them. And at her side, her husband who was back from the war in Afghanistan sang it. Luke, who had not yet lifted his voice in song, sang it with a strength and purity that resonated within her. Rebecca, who sat close to Luke, sang it, and Bishop Fischer and his wife, and Minister Yoder. And Minister Yoder's son Timothy, who closed his eyes as the words left his lips and the singing of the church families filled his ears.

*Stille Nacht, heilige Nacht,*
*Hirten erst kundgemacht*
*Durch der Engel Halleluja,*
*Tönt es laut von fern und nah:*
*Christ, der Retter ist da!*
*Christ, der Retter ist da!*

They sat in the parlor and in the kitchen, and the teens and children sat on the staircase and all along the hallway on the second floor. The candles in their hands were blown out or guttered out, and threads of white smoke raveled and unraveled in the air. The bishop prayed and thanked God and then extended his hand toward Micah.

"You are the new minister. Come, give us the Christmas message."

Micah was seated on a bench with Naomi. He shook his head. "No, no, it should be another."

"It is for you to do."

"But I don't have anything prepared."

"The Lord himself who has guided you this far will give you the words."

Naomi pushed him. "Go, go. When are you at a loss for words?"

Laughter moved back and forth in the rooms and up and down the stairs. Micah stood in front of the congregation and for a moment took in the light of the candles and lanterns and the woodstove on their hands and faces. He had no idea what to say. He still felt overwhelmed by the fact the church had chosen to embrace him rather than reject him. Then a verse made its way into his head.

"God bless you all. It's Christmas," he began, "and you have heard so many Christmas messages, what can I say to add to them? But I see Luke with us, and he is talking and singing, but a month ago he made no sound at all. I see Timothy, who two weeks ago was in a hospital bed in Philadelphia and fighting to sit up and eat. I see all of you when an hour ago I thought in my heart the church had split apart and was broken. And then I see myself standing here speaking with you, I who a week ago had no voice and no right to stand among you and worship. All of this astonishes me. Does it astonish you?"

Heads nodded. "*Ja, ja,*" people said softly.

"So I think that is the heart of the Christmas message. Nothing shall be impossible with God. Didn't the angel say that to Mary? Haven't many of you spoken the same words Mary did over the past few weeks, 'How can these things be?' Doesn't Gabriel give you and all of us here tonight the same message? Nothing shall be impossible with God. That is what has happened here among us. That is Christmas." He stopped to smile at his wife, whose face glowed in the fire from the woodstove. "The message I have is a lifelong message. Never lose heart and never forget that what is impossible for us is never impossible for the Lord. Never."

There was a silence. Then Minister Yoder began to lead out in an Amish hymn of praise in his deep voice. After a few moments women began to join in, and soon other men and the teens on the staircase as well. Bishop Fischer didn't sing with them, but lowered his head and listened. He thought it would end in a few minutes. But it went on, new voices coming in all the time, some high, some low, all harmonizing with one another, filling the house and all its rooms, filling his heart. He looked up as the hymn continued and saw Micah Bachman surrounded by his wife and Luke and Rebecca, by Minister Yoder and Timothy, by people who smiled and put their hands on his shoulders as they sang, by older women who hugged him and his wife.

*My Lord, so much has changed for the better, and yet for the great change to come so much had to be lost—our pride, our hardness of heart, our tradition, our unwillingness to bend, our reluctance to think something we did not understand could be from you. It has not been easy. It has not been without pain. But neither has it been without its own special glory. And it has been your doing.*

He looked at his people again, God's people, and at Micah Bachman as he sang, encircled by those same people.

*Sie, die mich ehren, werde ich ehren.* "*They that honor me I will honor.*"

"So sometimes God does," Bishop Fischer said quietly. "So sometimes love does."

**Murray Pura** earned his Master of Divinity degree from Acadia University in Wolfville, Nova Scotia, and his ThM degree in theology and interdisciplinary studies from Regent College in Vancouver, British Columbia. For more than 25 years, in addition to writing, he has pastored churches in Nova Scotia, British Columbia, and Alberta. Murray's writings have been short-listed for the Dartmouth Book Award, the  John Spencer Hill Literary Award, the Paraclete Fiction Award, and Toronto's Kobzar Literary Award. Murray pastors and writes in southern Alberta near the Rocky Mountains. He and his wife, Linda, have a son and a daughter.

Visit Murray's website at **www.murraypura.com**.

To learn more about Harvest House books and
to read sample chapters, log on to our website:

**www.harvesthousepublishers.com**

HARVEST HOUSE PUBLISHERS
EUGENE, OREGON

- Exclusive Book Previews
- Authentic Amish Recipes
- Q & A with Your Favorite Authors
- Free Downloads
- Author Interviews & Extras

# AmishReader.com

FOLLOW US:

Visit **AmishReader.com** today and
download your free copy of

## LASTING LOVE

a short story by Leslie Gould